THE STAR LOST

Michael Jan Friedman
WRITER

Peter Krause
PENCILLER

Pablo Marcos
INKER

LETTERED BY BOB PINAHA

COLORED BY JULIANNA FERRITER

ORIGINAL COVERS BY JEROME MOORE
INTRODUCTION BY RONALD D. MOORE

Based on STAR TREK: THE NEXT GENERATION created by Gene Roddenberry

STAR TREK: THE NEXT GENERATION THE STAR LOST

DC Comics, 1325 Avenue of the Americas, New York, NY 10019
A Division of Warner Bros. – A Time Warner Entertainment Company.
Printed in Canada. First Printing. ISBN #1-56389-084-4
Cover painting by Jason Palmer. Publication design by Veronica Carlin.

INTRODUCTION

By Ronald D. Moore

It's easy to get distracted in my office. Aside from the usual debris that seems to collect in any business, like memos, mail, and lazy colleagues, I have to contend with a collection of artifacts from another universe: the dedication plaque from the USS *Sutherland;* a set of cue cards used by James Doohan in "Relics"; an indecipherable placard from Kivas Fajo's ship; a large collection of scripts plotting out adventures old and new; a genuine black velvet painting of Elvis (identical to the one that I firmly believe adorns Worf's quarters somewhere off-camera); and a Darth Vader helmet.

I can sit at my desk and let my gaze wander over each of these items if I need a smile or a laugh or just a feeling of satisfaction. But there is one piece of memorabilia that never fails to evoke a somewhat deeper emotional response whenever it catches my eye. It sits high up on a shelf, perched alone on a space directly across from my desk with a commanding view of the entire room. It is the only item that not only brings a smile to my face, but simultaneously reminds me of where I came from and just how lucky I am to do what I do: it is an AMT model of the USS *Enterprise* that I built when I was twelve years old.

Everyone has a pet theory of why *Star Trek* is so popular after 25 years. People have written reams of material about the idealism inherent in Gene Roddenberry's universe, the relationship between the "final frontier" and the "New Frontier," the scientific plausibility of warp drive, the chemistry between the characters, the neat uniforms, the respect for the intelligence of the audience, Spock's ears, the sociological impact of pop culture on our national psyche, etc., etc.

I don't know why *Star Trek* is popular. I don't know why it grew beyond the confines of a weekly 1960s television series, or why it continues to grow and expand as it enters its second quarter century. All I know is what it meant to a young boy looking for heroes in a small town in central California. It meant a lot.

When I was growing up in the sleepy hamlet of Chowchilla (pop. 4,500) television provided me with a window on all the things that lay just beyond the cotton fields and almond orchards which surrounded the "city." As I looked through that window, I glimpsed a world that seemed to consist largely of picture-perfect families of six or more kids where no one was ever punished, astronauts and advertising executives who married women with magical powers, men from U.N.C.L.E., men who got Smart, hick Marines who never went to war, fun-loving prisoners in Nazi POW camps, Mod Squads...not a very inspiring group for a boy looking for someone to look up to. But then, somewhere around the third grade, I discovered a group of people whose only mission was to explore strange new worlds and boldly go where no man had gone before. I had found my heroes.

This was well before *Star Trek* had become a phenomenon. There were no movies, no conventions (none near me, anyway), no comics, no nothing. Just 79 episodes that somehow fired my imagination unlike anything else I'd seen. The starship *Enterprise* would pull up to my house at 5:00 pm every day and then whisk me away for an hour to some distant corner of the galaxy where a new adventure awaited. (At the tender age of nine I had yet to make a real distinction between "City on the Edge of Forever" and "Spock's Brain," but there would be plenty of time for that later.)

The crew of this mighty ship became my role models. I wanted to be as brave as Kirk, as logical as Spock, and as compassionate as McCoy. I laughed with them, cried with them, shouted with them, I even began to memorize arcane facts about them. (Go ahead. Ask me Kirk's serial number. I still know it.) They were people I could trust, people I could count on when I was feeling alone or when I was afraid to face another day of childhood. They were my friends and my companions and I loved every one of them.

Childhood passed into adolescence, and most of the things I loved as a child began to fall away. But not *Star Trek.* My affection for the show never flagged as I grew into a teenager and then an adult. The characters became old friends of mine...dependable, loyal, always there with an invitation for adventure if I needed a break from reality. They followed me from childhood in Chowchilla to college in Ithaca and finally to work in Los Angeles. No matter what I was doing, no matter what crummy little job I was slaving away at, I could always come home, turn on the VCR and let my old pals take me away for a while.

One day a new group of people came knocking at my door and asked to take me on some new voyages. They were a different bunch than my old friends: a bald Frenchman with a British accent, a pale-faced android, a Klingon (!), a touchy-feely Betazoid, a blind man, a punk kid, a red-haired doctor, a studly first officer, and a spunky security chief. I was cautious at first. They would have to earn my trust and my affection. So I watched and I waited...and I was not disappointed. These people were just as worthy of my respect and admiration as the old friends I'd known since childhood, and the ship they served aboard was a credit to her name.

Time passed and then a minor miracle happened. I sold a script... then a second script...and then I was hired as a staff writer on *The Next Generation.* It was as if my heroes had been watching me through those many years, waiting until I was ready, and then reached out and asked me to join them. I now sit in my office and write Captain's Logs and Stardates and warp factors and Klingons and make it so. Lou Gehrig wasn't the luckiest man on earth. I am.

I'm lucky because I get to do things like this. I get to introduce people like you to some friends of mine and let them take you for a ride. And *The Star Lost* is a great ride. It's full of derring-do and action-adventure with bizarre aliens, mysterious spaceships, and strange new worlds. But more than that, it is a story about people. It's about

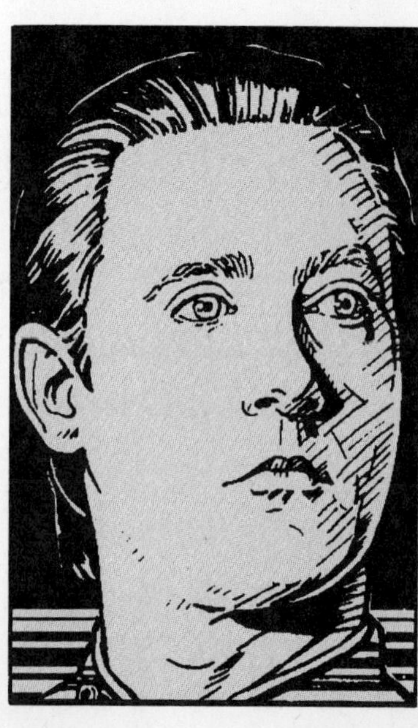

the ties that bind people together during a crisis and the spirit of hope that keeps them alive. It's about the need to believe in the people you love and about the need to let them go. It's about us. You and me. It's *Star Trek* at its best.

Far too many writers who try their hand at *Star Trek* see only the warp drive and the tricorders, but not the people who operate them. My friends aboard the *Enterprise* are more than just figures who press buttons and yell "Red Alert!" They are people, with hopes and dreams, flaws and insecurities, foibles and idiosyncrasies. If you can't find those voices and can't bring yourself to look beyond the uniforms and the technobabble, you'll never get to know these dear friends of mine and they won't take you on any real adventures. In *The Star Lost,* writer Michael Jan Friedman, penciller Peter Krause and inker Pablo Marcos, along with letterer Bob Pinaha and colorist Julianna Ferriter, have found those voices; and my friends have rewarded them with a real adventure.

This adventure starts with eight passengers aboard a shuttle as they set sail one day on a three-hour tour...a three-hour tour...—Sorry. Actually, this group of castaways never make it to an island, and they don't make radios out of coconuts, but I think you'll like it anyway.

To someone used to dealing with the constraints of a weekly television series, *The Star Lost* has a remarkable sweep and epic quality to it. Without the monetary considerations of TV, the creative team at DC Comics, under the sure hand of editor Bob Greenberger, has the ability to paint a story in far bolder strokes than we could ever hope to do on *TNG.* They can go to the water planet of Lanatos, swim around a bit, see the reactions of Mrs. Troi and Dr. Pulaski to somber news, meet the strange and gentle Skriiti, encounter a monstrous alien vessel, fight a rogues gallery of villains, and face down an entire Klingon battlefleet without having to worry about going over budget! I salivate at the thought.

I assume that almost everyone reading this book is a *Star Trek* fan of some degree, but there may be some among you who were given this by a Trekker friend, or you just liked the cover art, or you picked it up in order to kill some time. In that case, let me warn you: *Star Trek* is a hard habit to kick. It gets under your skin and infects your brain. Once you've seen Vulcan and Romulus, Argelius and Risa, it's hard to stay down on the farm. So if you find yourself tapping your chest and calling for a beam-up or asking a waiter for "Tea. Earl Grey. Hot," you can't say I didn't warn you. If you do decide to proceed, don't worry about the Klingons or the Romulans or the Lanatosian volcanoes—I know some people who will take good care of you. They know their way around the galaxy and they'll be sure to bring you home.

Let me introduce you to some friends of mine...

THE FEDERATION COLONY ON BETA HYDROS FOUR...
"ARE WE GOING TO DIE, MOMMA?"
NO, ALICIA, WE'RE NOT GOING TO DIE. WE'VE SENT FOR HELP.
WHAT KIND OF HELP?
REMEMBER THE BIG STARSHIP THAT BROUGHT US HERE? WELL, AN EVEN BIGGER ONE IS ON ITS WAY.
IT HAS DOCTORS-- LOTS OF DOCTORS. AND MEDICINES TO MAKE US FEEL BETTER.
HOW DO YOU KNOW THEY'RE COMING, MOMMA? CAN YOU SEE THEM?

NOT YET, HONEY. THEY'RE STILL A LITTLE TOO FAR AWAY. BUT THEY'RE FLYING HERE JUST AS FAST AS THEY CAN.
WHAT IF THEY CAN'T FIND US, MOMMA? THERE ARE SO MANY STARS... WHAT IF THEY GO TO THE WRONG ONE?
DON'T YOU WORRY ABOUT THAT.
THE BIG STARSHIP HAS MACHINES THAT CAN TELL THEM WHERE TO FIND US. IT CAN'T GET LOST NO MATTER WHAT.
YOU SURE?
VERY SURE. NOW. YOU GET SOME REST-- AND THE BIG SHIP WILL BE HERE BEFORE YOU KNOW IT.
ANY WORD, DOCTOR?
SURE. WE KEEP GETTING MESSAGES THAT THEY'RE ON THEIR WAY. BUT THERE'S STILL NO SIGN OF THEM.
I JUST TOLD MY LITTLE GIRL THAT NO ONE HERE WOULD DIE. I HOPE THE ENTERPRISE DOESN'T MAKE A LIAR OUT OF ME.

"CAPTAIN'S LOG, STARDATE 44212.9: WE CONTINUE TO PUSH OUR WARP ENGINES TO THE LIMIT AS WE APPROACH THE ALPHA AND BETA HYDROS STAR SYSTEMS.
"AT THE TIME OF OUR LAST COMMUNICATION WITH THE FEDERATION COLONIES THERE, THE ZELAZNAN FEVER WAS CLAIMING MORE AND MORE OF THEIR PEOPLE--BUT AS YET, THERE HAVE BEEN NO CASUALTIES...
NCC-1701-D
"...WITH ANY LUCK, WE WILL ARRIVE IN TIME TO KEEP IT THAT WAY."
THE FLIGHT OF THE Albert Einstein
MICHAEL JAN FRIEDMAN WRITER
PETER KRAUSE PENCILLER
PABLO MARCOS INKER
BOB PINAHA LETTERER
JULIANNA FERRITER COLORIST
ROBERT GREENBERGER~ EDITOR
BASED ON STAR TREK: THE NEXT GENERATION CREATED BY GENE RODDENBERRY

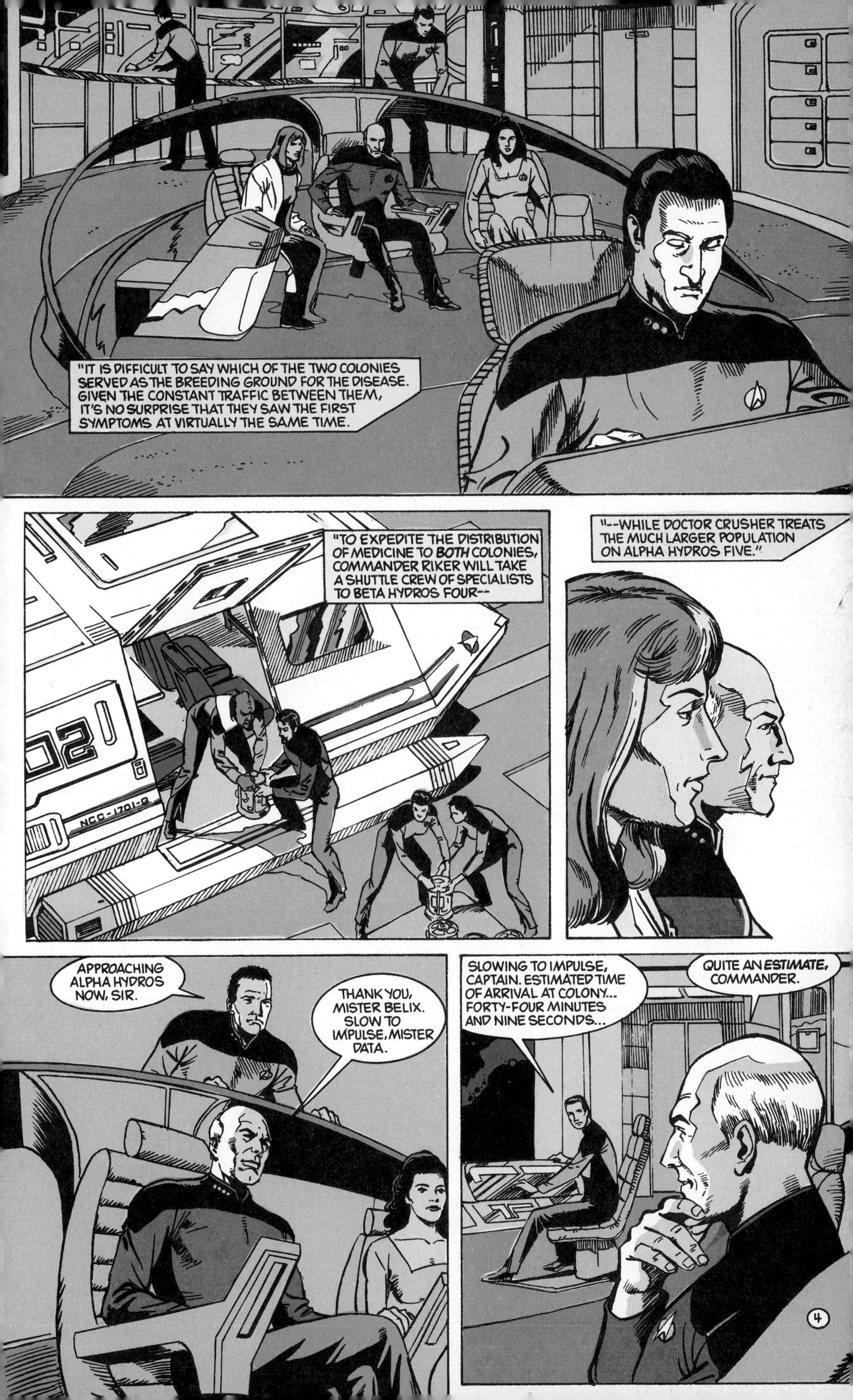

"IT IS DIFFICULT TO SAY WHICH OF THE TWO COLONIES SERVED AS THE BREEDING GROUND FOR THE DISEASE. GIVEN THE CONSTANT TRAFFIC BETWEEN THEM, IT'S NO SURPRISE THAT THEY SAW THE FIRST SYMPTOMS AT VIRTUALLY THE SAME TIME.

"TO EXPEDITE THE DISTRIBUTION OF MEDICINE TO *BOTH* COLONIES, COMMANDER RIKER WILL TAKE A SHUTTLE CREW OF SPECIALISTS TO BETA HYDROS FOUR--

COMMANDER RIKER--HOW IS IT GOING DOWN THERE?
ACCORDING TO SCHEDULE, SIR.

WE'RE ALL PACKED AND READY TO GO.
EXCELLENT. AND GOOD LUCK, NUMBER ONE.

I DON'T EXPECT WE'LL NEED ANY LUCK, CAPTAIN. THIS IS ABOUT AS STRAIGHTFORWARD A MISSION AS I'VE SEEN IN A LONG TIME.
IT *MUST* BE-- IF THE CAPTAIN LET *ME* GO ALONG.
YOU'VE GOT TO WALK BEFORE YOU CAN RUN, MISTER CRUSHER.

AT LEAST YOU'LL KEEP BUSY PILOTING THE SHUTTLE. THE REST OF US WILL BE TWIDDLING OUR THUMBS ALL THE WAY TO BETA HYDROS.
NCC-1701-D
02

SPEAK FOR YOURSELF, COMMANDER. VULCANS DO NOT *TWIDDLE*.

OH? AND WHAT DO YOU DO TO PASS THE TIME?
NORMALLY, WE ENGAGE IN MEDITATION.

CONGRATULATIONS, DOCTOR SELAR. YOU'VE JUST SUCCEEDED IN MAKING TWIDDLING SOUND EXCITING.

EXCUSE ME FOR SAYING SO, BUT IS THIS THE TIME FOR JOKING? WHILE INNOCENT PEOPLE ARE SUFFERING ON BETA HYDROS FOUR?

LET ME GIVE YOU SOME ADVICE, FARADAY. WHEN WE GET TO THE COLONY, WE'LL HAVE A PRETTY GRUELING SCHEDULE. THERE WON'T BE ANY TIME FOR JOKING THEN.

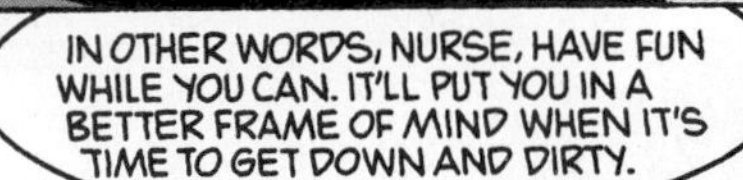
IN OTHER WORDS, NURSE, HAVE FUN WHILE YOU CAN. IT'LL PUT YOU IN A BETTER FRAME OF MIND WHEN IT'S TIME TO GET DOWN AND DIRTY.

TWO MINUTES TO DEPARTURE, SIR.
ACKNOWLEDGED, ENSIGN.

I HOPE THAT HATCH IS CLOSED TIGHT, LIEUTENANT. SHUTTLES ARE NOT MY FAVORITE MEANS OF TRANSPORTATION.

THIS VESSEL IS SECURE, DOCTOR MARINO. I HAVE CHECKED IT MYSELF.

SORRY, LIEUTENANT. I DIDN'T MEAN TO IMPLY OTHERWISE.

DON'T TELL ME YOU'VE NEVER TRAVELED IN A SHUTTLE, DOCTOR.
NEVER.

WELL, YOU'RE IN GOOD HANDS. FROM WHAT I UNDERSTAND, ENSIGN CRUSHER IS ONE OF THE BEST PILOTS AROUND.

NOT TRUE. HE IS THE BEST PILOT AROUND.

YOU'RE GOING TO GIVE ME A SWELLED HEAD, SIR.

"CAPTAIN'S LOG, SUPPLEMENTAL: HAVING SENT THE EINSTEIN ON ITS WAY, WE ARE ENTERING ORBIT AROUND ALPHA HYDROS FIVE.
"NOR ARE WE A MOMENT TOO SOON, JUDGING BY THE REPORTS WE'VE RECEIVED FROM THE COLONISTS."
"FORTUNATELY, DOCTOR CRUSHER HAS DONE THIS SORT OF THING BEFORE. THE COLONISTS COULD NOT BE IN MORE CAPABLE HANDS."
ALL RIGHT, EVERYONE. YOU KNOW WHAT TO DO.
THEY'RE HERE!
THANK GOD!

WILL SHE BE ALL RIGHT, DOCTOR?
ABSOLUTELY. IT'S JUST GOING TO TAKE A LITTLE TIME--AND A LITTLE CARE.

WHY DON'T YOU GET SOME REST? WE CAN TAKE IT FROM HERE--REALLY WE CAN.

HOW MAY I BE OF SERVICE, DOCTOR?
YOU CAN START BY DISTRIBUTING THOSE CONTAINERS, DATA.

I'M SURE OUR FRIENDS THERE CAN USE A HAND.

IT COULD HAVE BEEN A *LOT* WORSE.

I THINK THE COLONISTS EXAGGERATED THE SEVERITY OF THE SYMPTOMS. BUT THEN, THAT'S NORMAL.
IF THE OTHER COLONY IS IN NO WORSE SHAPE THAN THIS ONE, COMMANDER RIKER WILL BE BACK IN NO TIME.

ARE YOU SURE, COMMANDER?

I'M SURE, ENSIGN. THOUGH UNDER OTHER CIRCUMSTANCES, I'D BE ONLY TOO GLAD TO PULL UP A CHAIR.

WE DO HAVE SOME TIME BEFORE WE GET TO BETA HYDROS. AND IT'S NOT AS IF I NEED YOU UP HERE.
EVEN SO...

WHEN I'M COMMANDING A MISSION, I LIKE TO HAVE MY WITS ABOUT ME. NO DISTRACTIONS.
AND POKER CAN BE VERY DISTRACTING.

YOU ARE TAKING AN INORDINATE AMOUNT OF TIME, DOCTOR.
I TOLD YOU, LIEUTENANT-- I LIKE TO EXAMINE ALL THE ANGLES.

THIS IS NOT SURGERY, DOCTOR. IT IS ONLY A POKER GAME.

NOT MUCH OF A POKER PLAYER, DOCTOR?
THE GAME HAS NEVER HELD MUCH INTEREST FOR ME.
I AM MORE PARTIAL TO CHESS OR KNACKLES-- GAMES WHERE LUCK IS NOT A FACTOR.
YOU WOULDN'T HAVE GOTTEN ALONG VERY WELL WITH MY GRANDMOTHER. SHE TOLD ME THAT NOTHING IS MORE IMPORTANT THAN LUCK. IN FACT--
WHAT THE--?
MY GOD!
STEADY, WES!
BUT WHAT IS IT?
NEVER MIND THAT NOW.

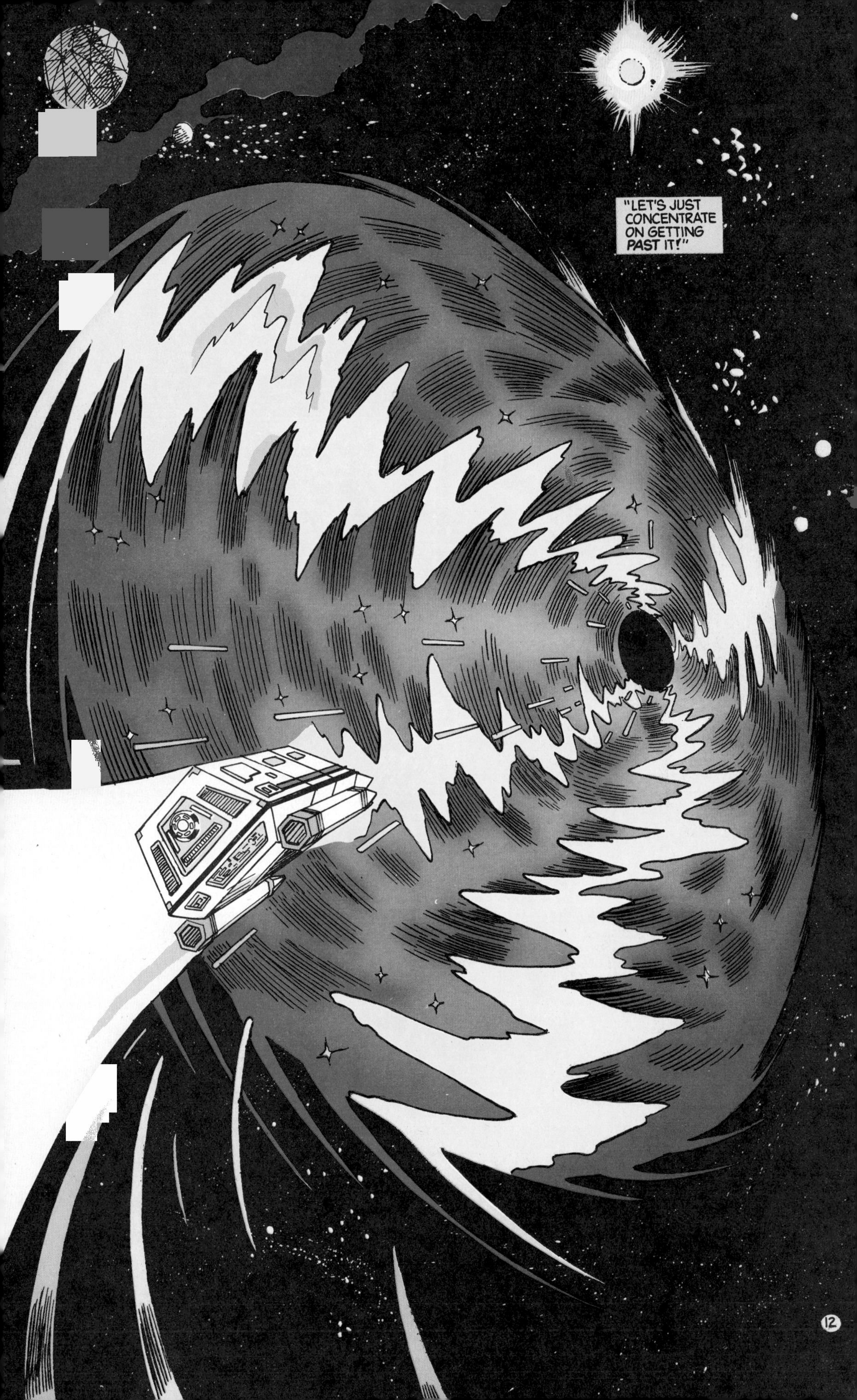
"LET'S JUST CONCENTRATE ON GETTING PAST IT!"

I'M TRYING, SIR--BUT IT SEEMS TO BE GETTING BIGGER!
REVERSE ENGINES!

"REVERSING THEM, COMMANDER--BUT IT'S NOT DOING ANY GOOD! THAT THING IS SUCKING US IN!"

SECURE THE DECK--IT LOOKS LIKE THE RIDE'S GOING TO GET *ROUGH* FROM HERE ON IN!
ENSIGN CRUSHER--ALL POWER TO THE SHIELDS!

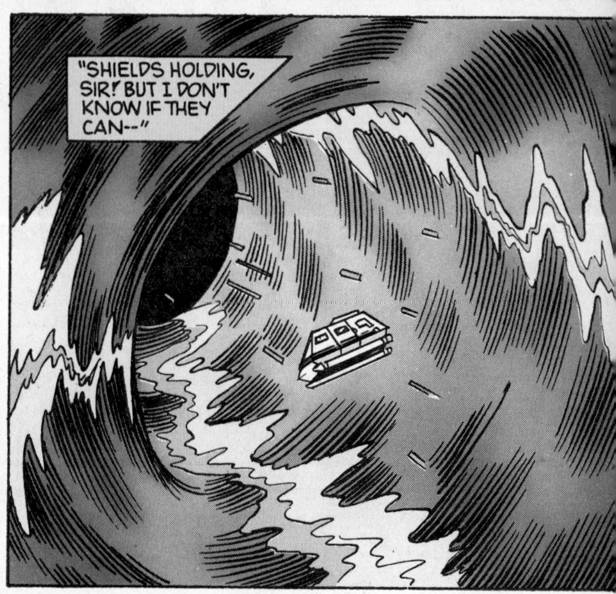
"SHIELDS HOLDING, SIR! BUT I DON'T KNOW IF THEY CAN--"

RRRGH!

WHAT HAPPENED?
IS EVERYONE ALL RIGHT?

COMMANDER! COMMANDER!

HE IS ALIVE--BUT JUST BARELY. HIS ALPHA LEVELS SUGGEST SEVERE TRAUMA.

FARADAY--DIMETHADRINE, ON THE DOUBLE.
GOLD--SOMETHING FOR THE SHOCK.

PROGNOSIS, DOCTOR?

IT IS TOO EARLY TO TELL, LIEUTENANT. BUT WE'RE DOING EVERYTHING WE CAN.

SIR--WE SEEM TO HAVE LOST THE *EINSTEIN'S* SIGNAL!

THEY SHOULD STILL BE IN RANGE, CAPTAIN. BUT FOR SOME REASON, THEY'VE STOPPED TRANSMITTING!

TRY ANOTHER FREQUENCY, MISTER BELIX.
I'M RUNNING THROUGH **ALL** FREQUENCIES, SIR. BUT THERE'S STILL NO ANSWER.

BLAST.

"MISTER CHRISTOPHER, CHART A COURSE FOR BETA HYDROS FOUR. AS SOON AS WE'RE FINISHED HERE, I WANT TO CHECK UP ON OUR SHUTTLE..."

...MORE THAN LIKELY, IT'S JUST AN EQUIPMENT MALFUNCTION. BUT JUST TO BE SURE...

HE'S STABLE.

BUT FOR HOW LONG?
THAT IS ANYONE'S GUESS, AT THIS POINT.

HOW IS HE?
HIS INJURY WAS CONSIDERABLE. BUT FOR NOW, HE FEELS NO PAIN.

COMMANDER RIKER IS THE REASON I SIGNED ON BOARD THE ENTERPRISE. I'D HEARD SO MUCH ABOUT HIM...

...AND NOW, TO SEE HIM LIKE THIS... I WISH THERE WERE SOMETHING I COULD DO.

DON'T WE ALL, ENSIGN. DON'T WE ALL.

IT'S NO USE, SIR. NONE OF THESE CONFIGURATIONS LOOK FAMILIAR.

THAT VORTEX WE RAN INTO COULD HAVE DEPOSITED US ANYWHERE.

AND WITHOUT A FAMILIAR REFERENCE POINT, WE CAN'T RETURN TO FEDERATION SPACE-- MUCH LESS COMPLETE OUR MISSION TO BETA HYDROS.

I HEARD THAT, LIEUTENANT. ARE YOU SAYING THAT WE CAN'T GET HOME?

WE WILL FIND A WAY HOME, DOCTOR. IT IS ONLY A MATTER OF WHEN-- AND HOW.

"UH-OH. MORE BAD NEWS..."
"WHAT'S THAT?"

...OUR STAR DRIVE IS BURNED OUT. MAYBE WHEN WE TRIED TO REVERSE ENGINES AGAINST THE VORTEX... I DON'T KNOW.

CAN'T WE REPAIR IT?
NOT LIKELY, SIR. WE DON'T HAVE THE TOOLS--OR THE PARTS.

SO EVEN IF WE CAN FIGURE OUT WHERE WE ARE--WE'LL HAVE TO HEAD HOME AT IMPULSE SPEED.
WE COULD BE OLD AND GREY BEFORE WE EVEN GET NEAR FEDERATION TERRITORY!

YOU HEAR WHAT THEY'RE SAYING, DOCTOR?
MY HEARING IS QUITE GOOD, NURSE. I CANNOT HELP BUT HEAR IT.

DOCTOR... WE COULD BE LOST. FOREVER. DOESN'T THAT BOTHER YOU?
OF COURSE IT DOES.

BUT THERE IS NOTHING YOU OR I CAN DO TO IMPROVE THE SITUATION--SO IS IT LOGICAL TO DWELL ON IT?

ON THE OTHER HAND, COMMANDER RIKER'S CONDITION IS SOMETHING WE **CAN** DO SOMETHING ABOUT. LET US TRY TO FOCUS ON THAT FACT--AND IGNORE EXTRANEOUS DATA.

ENOUGH! CHATTERING LIKE MONKEYS WILL GET US NOWHERE!

WE ARE STILL ALIVE. WE STILL HAVE FOOD AND LIFE SUPPORT. WE STILL HAVE OUR **WITS**!

YOU'RE RIGHT, LIEUTENANT. WHERE THERE'S A WILL, THERE'S A WAY-- RIGHT?

WELL PUT, ENSIGN NIGATA. AND NOW, WE WILL NEED A PLAN...

MY GOD.

THE BETA HYDROS COLONY HAS CONFIRMED IT. THE SHUTTLE NEVER ARRIVED.

BUT... HOW? WHAT COULD HAVE HAPPENED?

WE'RE TRYING TO DETERMINE THAT NOW. AND I HAVE BY NO MEANS GIVEN THEM UP FOR...

FOR *DEAD*, JEAN-LUC? IT'S ALL RIGHT. YOU CAN SAY IT.

JUST DON'T LET IT TURN OUT TO BE *TRUE*.

I APPRECIATE THAT. NOW, IF YOU'LL EXCUSE ME, I'VE GOT TO BRIEF MY STAFF. THEY DON'T KNOW YET THAT THE BETA HYDROS COLONY STILL NEEDS HELP.
OF COURSE, DOCTOR.
"CAPTAIN'S PERSONAL LOG: I HAVE INFORMED DOCTOR CRUSHER OF HER SON'S DISAPPEARANCE. IN SOME WAYS, SHE IS TAKING IT BETTER THAN I AM.
BAM
"IT'S BEEN OVER TEN YEARS SINCE I HAD TO TELL HER OF HER HUSBAND'S DEATH. IT WAS THE HARDEST THING I'VE EVER DONE.
"NOW, I FACE THE PROSPECT OF BEING THE BEARER OF BAD NEWS AGAIN. WORSE NEWS--THE WORST A MOTHER CAN IMAGINE.
"I WISH IT WERE ME ON THAT SHUTTLE INSTEAD OF WESLEY. I WOULD SOONER FACE DEATH MYSELF THAN HAVE TO WITNESS BEVERLY CRUSHER'S PAIN A SECOND TIME."

DEANNA...

IT'S TRUE-- ISN'T IT?

YES, IT IS. THE SHUTTLE IS MISSING WITHOUT A TRACE.
THEN ALL THOSE PEOPLE...COMMANDER RIKER AND THE OTHERS...

NO ONE'S MORE RESOURCEFUL THAN WILL RIKER, COMMANDER. WE MUST HAVE FAITH.

YEAH. SURE. WHATEVER YOU SAY.

WE COULD JUST SIT HERE AND WAIT FOR HELP TO FIND US. BUT IT'S PRETTY UNLIKELY THAT WE'LL BE FOUND.
OUR BEST BET IS TO JUST PICK A HEADING AT RANDOM--AND PURSUE IT AT FULL IMPULSE. AT LEAST THAT WAY, WE'VE GOT A *CHANCE* OF GETTING HOME AGAIN.

BUT WHAT IF IT'S THE *WRONG* HEADING? WHAT IF WE'RE JUST GETTING FARTHER AND FARTHER AWAY?

WE MUST TAKE THAT CHANCE. NOT ONLY FOR OURSELVES-- BUT FOR COMMANDER RIKER.

LIEUTENANT WORF IS RIGHT. THERE IS ONLY SO MUCH I CAN DO FOR HIM HERE.
IF WE DON'T GET HIM TO A FULLY-EQUIPPED MEDICAL FACILITY SOON, HE MAY DIE.

I AM THE RANKING OFFICER HERE. IT IS *MY* DECISION.

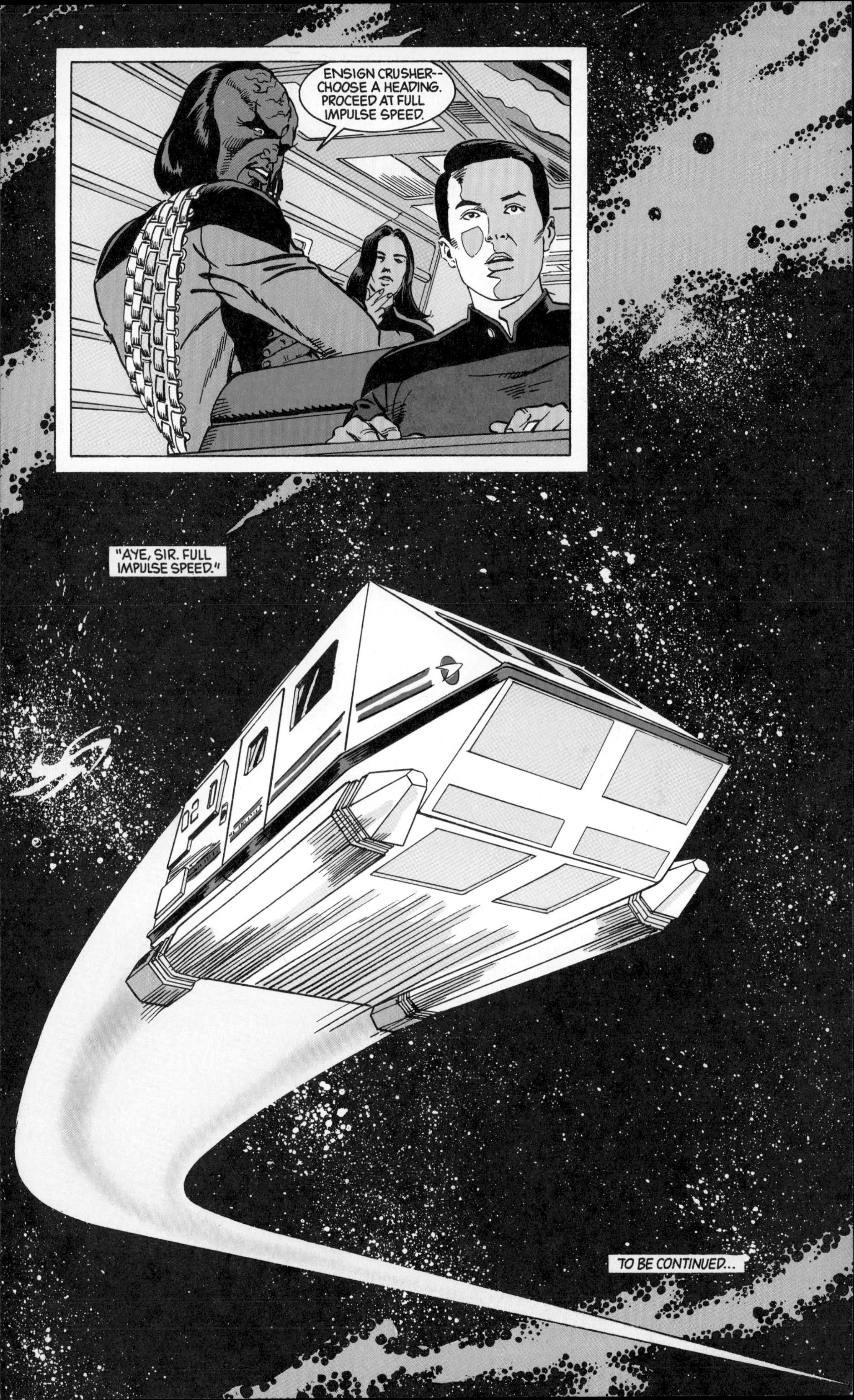

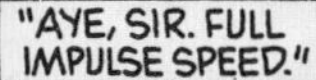

TO BE CONTINUED...

Mourning
STAR
"CAPTAIN'S PERSONAL LOG, STARDATE 442953 I HAVE TRIED MY BEST TO BELIEVE IT--TO GIVE IN TO THE INEVITABLE CONCLUSION THAT THE SHUTTLE EINSTEIN, WITH ITS CREW OF EIGHT SKILLED AND DEDICATED PEOPLE, HAS BEEN IRRETRIEVABLY LOST.
"BUT I DO NOT BELIEVE IT. PERHAPS I NEVER WILL.
"NONETHELESS, AFTER DAYS OF FUTILITY AND FRUSTRATION, I CAN NO LONGER JUSTIFY TO STARFLEET THE USE OF THE ENTERPRISE AS A SEARCH VESSEL. NOR CAN I ASK MY CREW TO SHARE MY UNLIKELY HOPES. FOR THEIR SAKE, I MUST PUT TO REST THE MEMORIES OF THOSE WHO DISAPPEARED WITH THE EINSTEIN."
MICHAEL JAN FRIEDMAN WRITER
PETER KRAUSE PENCILLER
PABLO MARCOS INKER
BOB PINAHA LETTERER
JULIANNA FERRITER COLORIST
ROBERT GREENBERGER EDITOR
BASED ON STAR TREK: THE NEXT GENERATION CREATED BY GENE RODDENBERRY

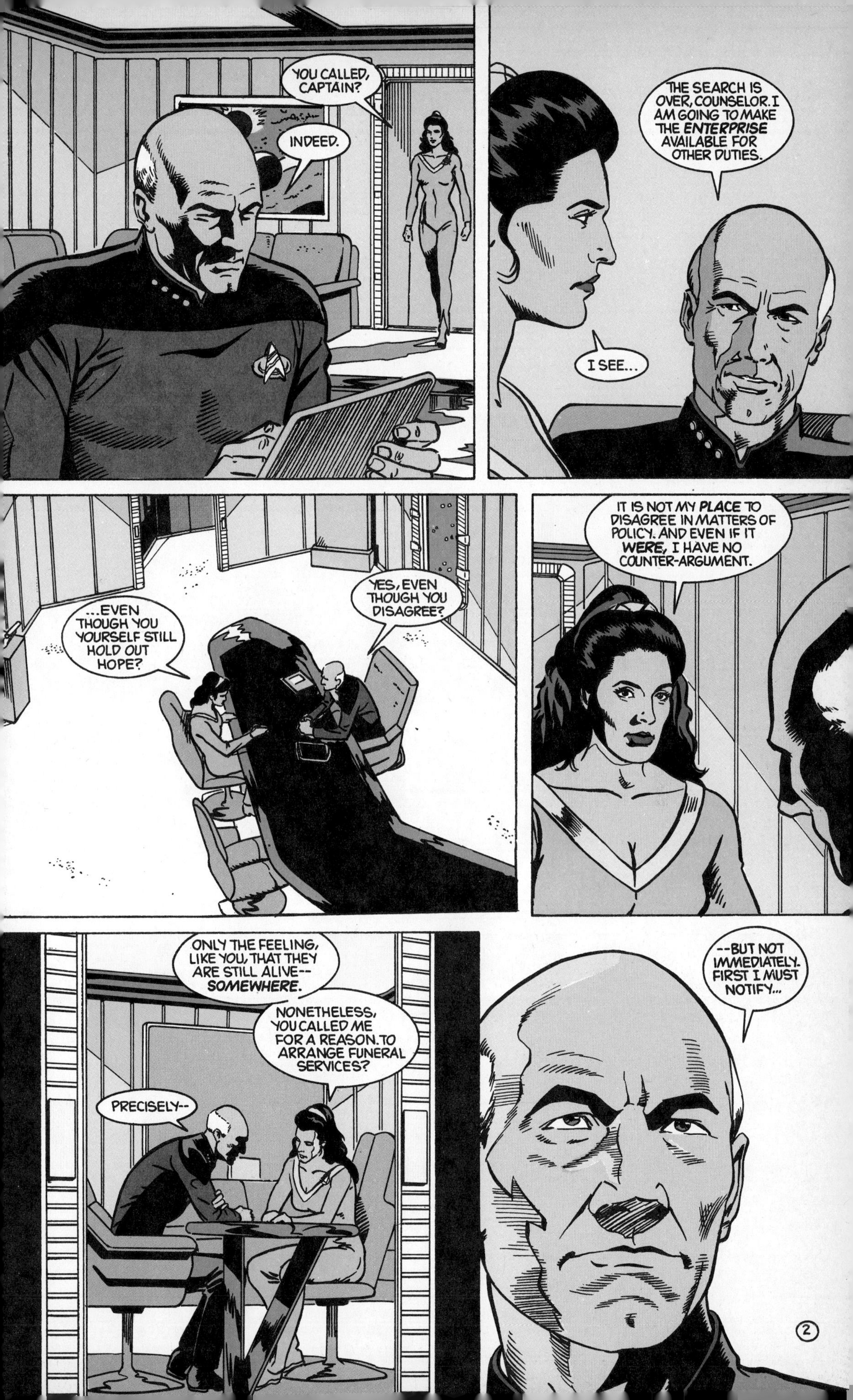

YOU CALLED, CAPTAIN?
INDEED.

THE SEARCH IS OVER, COUNSELOR. I AM GOING TO MAKE THE ***ENTERPRISE*** AVAILABLE FOR OTHER DUTIES.
I SEE...

"...THE NEXT-OF-KIN."

WHO IS IT?
IT IS I, BEVERLY.

08
CMO BEVERLY CRUSHER

COME IN, JEAN-LUC. PLEASE.

BEVERLY, I--
DON'T SAY IT, JEAN-LUC.

THERE'S NO NEED. I CAN SEE IT IN YOUR FACE.

I WISH THERE WERE SOME WAY TO EXPRESS MY SYMPATHY...
I KNOW. REMEMBER, WE'VE BEEN THROUGH THIS BEFORE.

AND I SWORE THAT I WOULD NEVER GO THROUGH IT AGAIN-- NOT WITH YOU.
I NEVER SHOULD HAVE LET HIM BOARD THAT BLASTED SHUTTLECRAFT!

AND WHAT THEN? IF IT HADN'T BEEN WESLEY, IT WOULD HAVE BEEN SOMEONE ELSE. AND THEN YOU'D BE STANDING AT HIS MOTHER'S DOOR, OR HIS WIFE'S, WITH THE SAME TERRIBLE CHORE TO PERFORM.

WESLEY KNEW WHAT HE WAS GETTING INTO. HE KNEW BETTER THAN MOST YOUNG MEN, AFTER WHAT HAPPENED TO HIS FATHER.
AND HE STILL WANTED IT--RISKS AND ALL.
4

IF HE'S DEAD, HE DIED HELPING OTHERS. ISN'T THAT THE BEST WAY? THE ONLY WAY, REALLY, FOR THOSE OF US WHO GO OUT INTO SPACE?
I'M PROUD OF THE PERSON HE GREW UP TO BE. OF WHAT HE MADE OF HIMSELF.
I'LL ALWAYS HAVE THAT. AND NOBODY CAN TAKE IT AWAY FROM ME.
YOU'RE A VERY SPECIAL WOMAN, BEVERLY. A VERY SPECIAL WOMAN.
I MUST GO NOW. BUT I'LL BE BACK. TO TALK... IF YOU LIKE, THAT IS.
CERTAINLY.
5

NOTHING.
YOU MEAN STILL NOTHING.

I MEAN NOTHING YET. WE'VE GOT TO HAVE A POSITIVE ATTITUDE ABOUT THIS.

SORRY. IT'S JUST THAT THE... THE WAITING IS GETTING TO ME.
AND I KEEP THINKING... WHAT IF WE NEVER FIND OUR WAY BACK?

I MEAN, ARE WE GOING TO LIVE OUT OUR LIVES IN THIS THING? IS THIS THE ONLY WORLD WE'RE EVER GOING TO KNOW?
NCC-1701-D
02

I DID IT. EVEN AT IMPULSE SPEED, WE MAY BE ABLE TO FIND A CLASS M PLANET EVENTUALLY. THAT IS, IF WE DECIDE THAT WE'RE NOT GOING TO--

--DAMN. NOW YOU'VE GOT ME DOING IT!

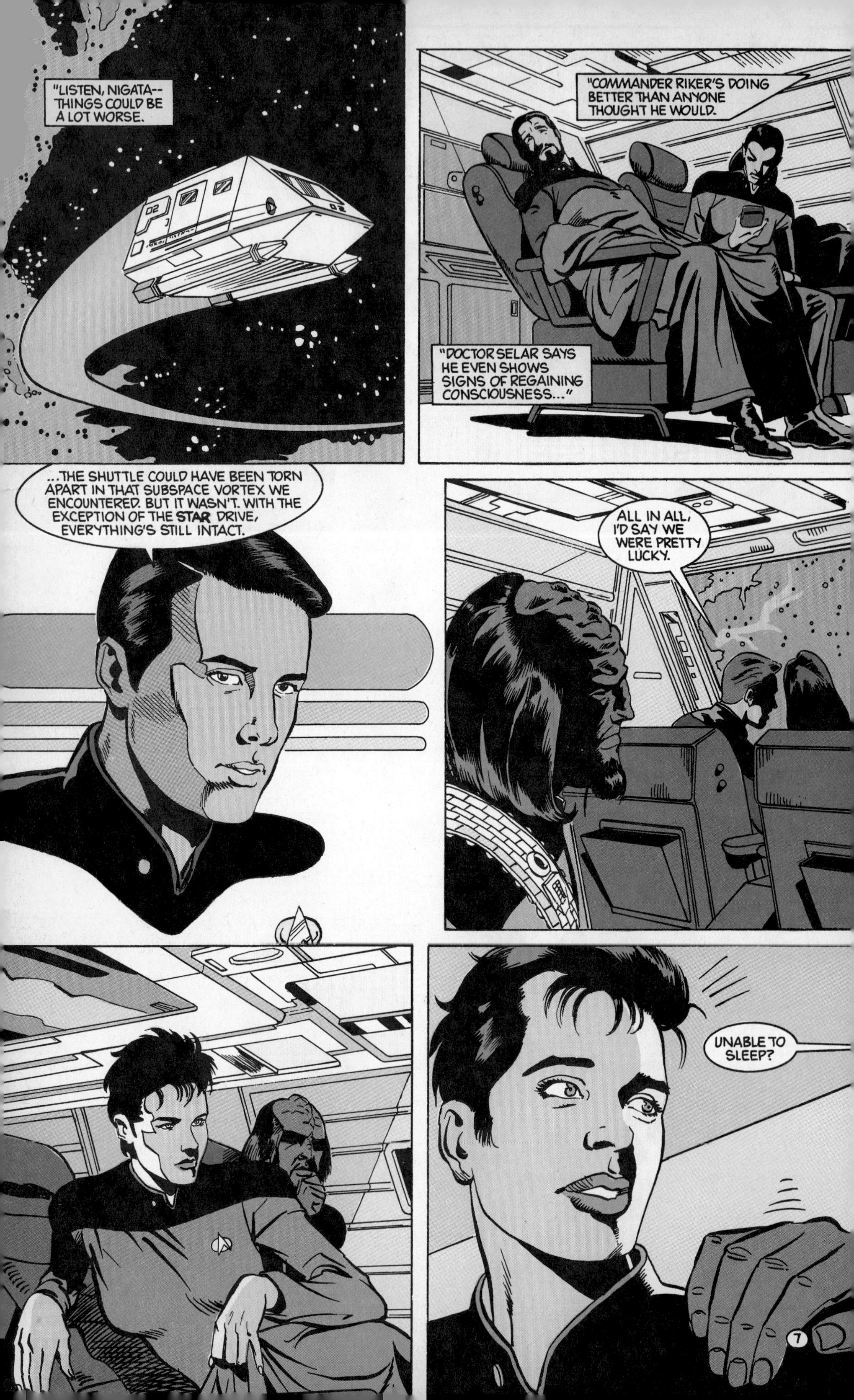

"LISTEN, NIGATA--
THINGS COULD BE
A LOT WORSE.

"COMMANDER RIKER'S DOING
BETTER THAN ANYONE
THOUGHT HE WOULD.

"DOCTOR SELAR SAYS
HE EVEN SHOWS
SIGNS OF REGAINING
CONSCIOUSNESS..."

...THE SHUTTLE COULD HAVE BEEN TORN
APART IN THAT SUBSPACE VORTEX WE
ENCOUNTERED. BUT IT WASN'T. WITH THE
EXCEPTION OF THE **STAR** DRIVE,
EVERYTHING'S STILL INTACT.

ALL IN ALL,
I'D SAY WE
WERE PRETTY
LUCKY.

TOO MUCH TO THINK ABOUT, I GUESS. AND MAYBE A FEW TOO MANY REGRETS.
REGRETS? YOU SPEAK AS IF YOUR LIFE WERE OVER.
DID YOU NOT HEAR WHAT ENSIGN CRUSHER SAID? THIS IS A TIME FOR COURAGE, NOT DESPAIR.
EASY FOR YOU TO SAY, LIEUTENANT. BUT I DON'T FEEL VERY COURAGEOUS RIGHT NOW. IN FACT, I'M DOWN-RIGHT SCARED.
COURAGE IS **RESISTANCE** TO FEAR, NURSE FARADAY. **MASTERY** OF FEAR--NOT **ABSENCE** OF FEAR.
IS THAT A **KLINGON** SAYING, SIR?
NCC-1701-D
02

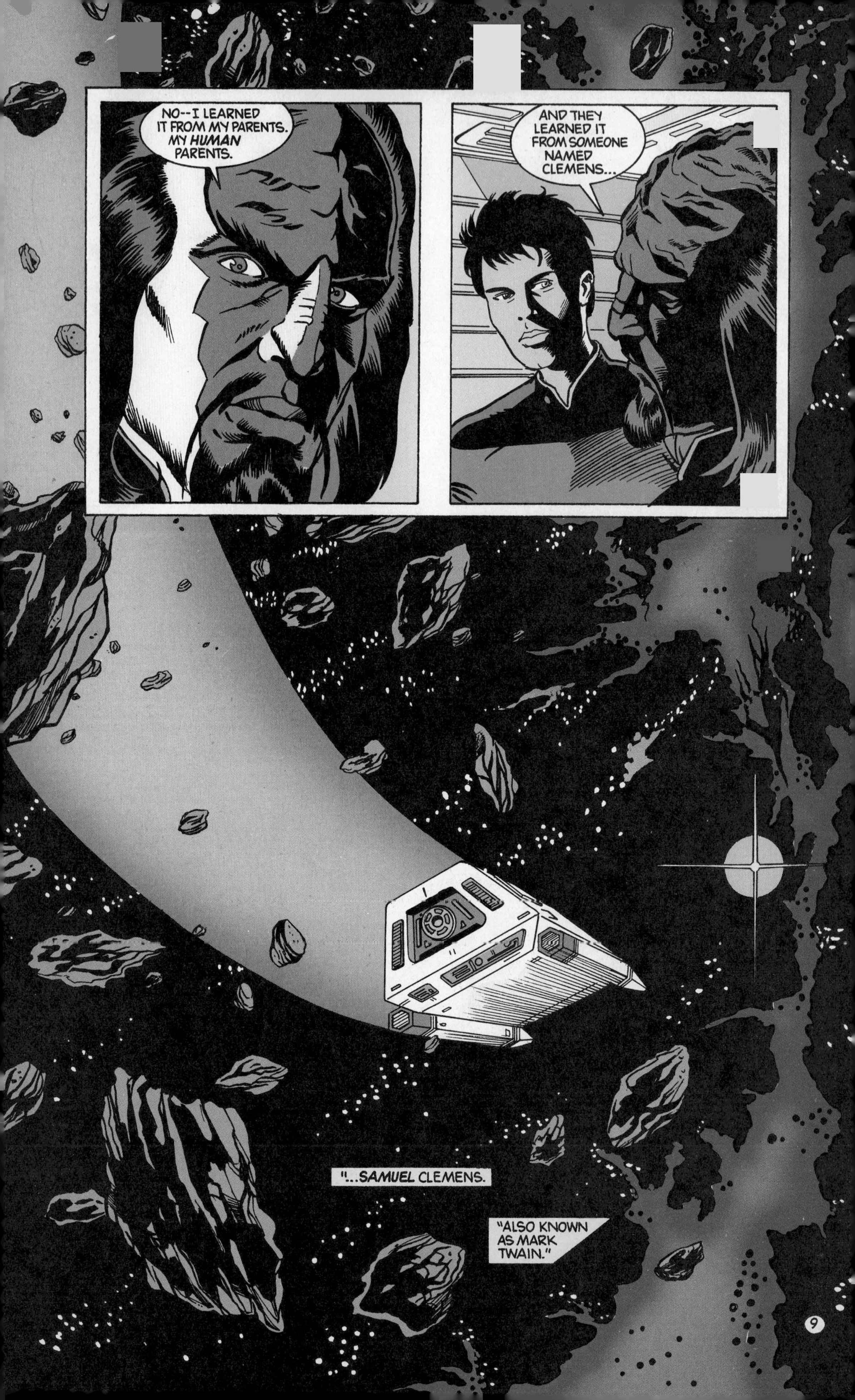

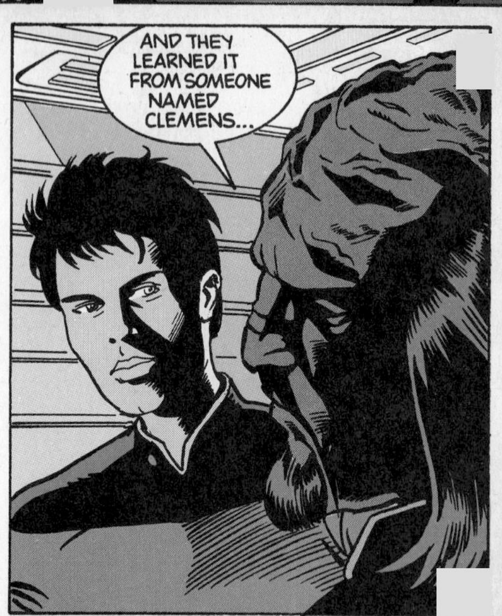

"...*SAMUEL* CLEMENS.

"ALSO KNOWN AS MARK TWAIN."

IT ISN'T UNTIL SOMEONE IS GONE THAT YOU REALIZE HOW LITTLE YOU KNEW ABOUT HIM.
10

WILL RIKER STOOD AT MY SIDE EVERY DAY FOR THE LAST THREE AND A HALF YEARS. AND TO BE SURE, IN THAT TIME I LEARNED MUCH OF HIS LIKES AND DISLIKES...
...I LEARNED THAT HE HAD AN AFFECTION FOR NEW ORLEANS JAZZ AND PERFECT OMELETS AND ALASKAN PINE FORESTS...
...AND THAT HE LOVED A GOOD JOKE.
I LEARNED OF HIS MOTHER, WHOSE MEMORY WAS HIS MOST CHERISHED POSSESSION. AND I HAD THE OPPORTUNITY TO MEET HIS FATHER FIRSTHAND.
I LEARNED THAT HE PUT THE SAFETY OF THIS SHIP AND ITS CREW BEFORE HIS OWN. AND THAT "DUTY" WAS MORE THAN JUST A WORD TO HIM.
BUT HOW WELL DID I REALLY KNOW WILL RIKER? HOW MUCH MORE MIGHT I HAVE LEARNED IF HE HAD NOT PERISHED IN THE SERVICE OF OTHERS?
STARFLEET HAS LOST ONE OF ITS FINEST OFFICERS. BUT I HAVE LOST A FRIEND.

WORF WAS NOT THE EASIEST PERSON TO GET CLOSE TO. OR TO PLEASE.
AFTER ALL, HE WAS A KLINGON. AND KLINGONS PRIDE THEMSELVES ON THEIR INDEPENDENCE--THEIR HIGH, SOMETIMES PAINFULLY HIGH STANDARDS.
BUT I CAN TELL YOU, WITHOUT GIVING AWAY ANY CONFIDENCES, THAT HE WAS PROUD OF THIS SHIP. PROUD TO SERVE ON HER, AND PROUD OF THE PEOPLE HE SERVED ALONGSIDE.
AND SOMETIMES, HIS EMOTIONS WENT BEYOND PRIDE. SOMETIMES THEY COULD ONLY BE DESCRIBED AS LOVE--FIERCE AND POWERFUL AND UNRELENTING--THOUGH HE HIMSELF WOULD HAVE DENIED THE APPLICABILITY OF THE WORD.
WE MAY NEVER KNOW WHAT HAPPENED TO THE EINSTEIN. BUT ONE THING IS CERTAIN...
...WORF MET HIS FATE SQUARELY AND BRAVELY, AND IN A MANNER THAT WOULD HAVE PLEASED HIS ANCESTORS.

I WISH I WERE BETTER WITH WORDS. I WISH I COULD COME UP WITH SOMETHING POETIC--THE KIND OF EPITAPH THAT WESLEY CRUSHER DESERVED.
BUT SINCE I CAN'T, LET ME SHARE A MEMORY WITH YOU. NOT A STORY EXACTLY--JUST A PICTURE THAT'S STUCK IN MY MEMORY.
WESLEY'S SITTING CROSS-LEGGED ON THE CATWALK IN ENGINEERING. HE'S GOT A FREQUENCY MODULATOR ON THE FLOOR IN FRONT OF HIM.
THE FREQUENCY MODULATOR IS IN PIECES. AND WESLEY'S STUDYING THEM--NOT MOVING, JUST STUDYING THEM.
THERE'S A LIGHT IN HIS EYES--OR MAYBE IT'S NOT A LIGHT, BUT IT SURE LOOKED LIKE ONE THROUGH THIS *VISOR* OF MINE.
AND HE'S HAPPY. HE'S COMPLETELY AND UTTERLY *HAPPY*.
THAT'S THE WAY I'M GOING TO REMEMBER HIM.
13

TO: KYLE RIKER
DIPLOMATIC CORPS
REGRET TO INFORM
YOU THAT WILLIAM RIKER
COMMANDER U.S.S.
ENTERPRISE HAS BEEN
REPORTED MISSING
STARFLEET
EXTENDS ITS HEART
FELT CONDOLENCES
MY GOD, WILL...
...I JUST GOT YOU BACK--AND NOW YOU'RE GONE AGAIN...

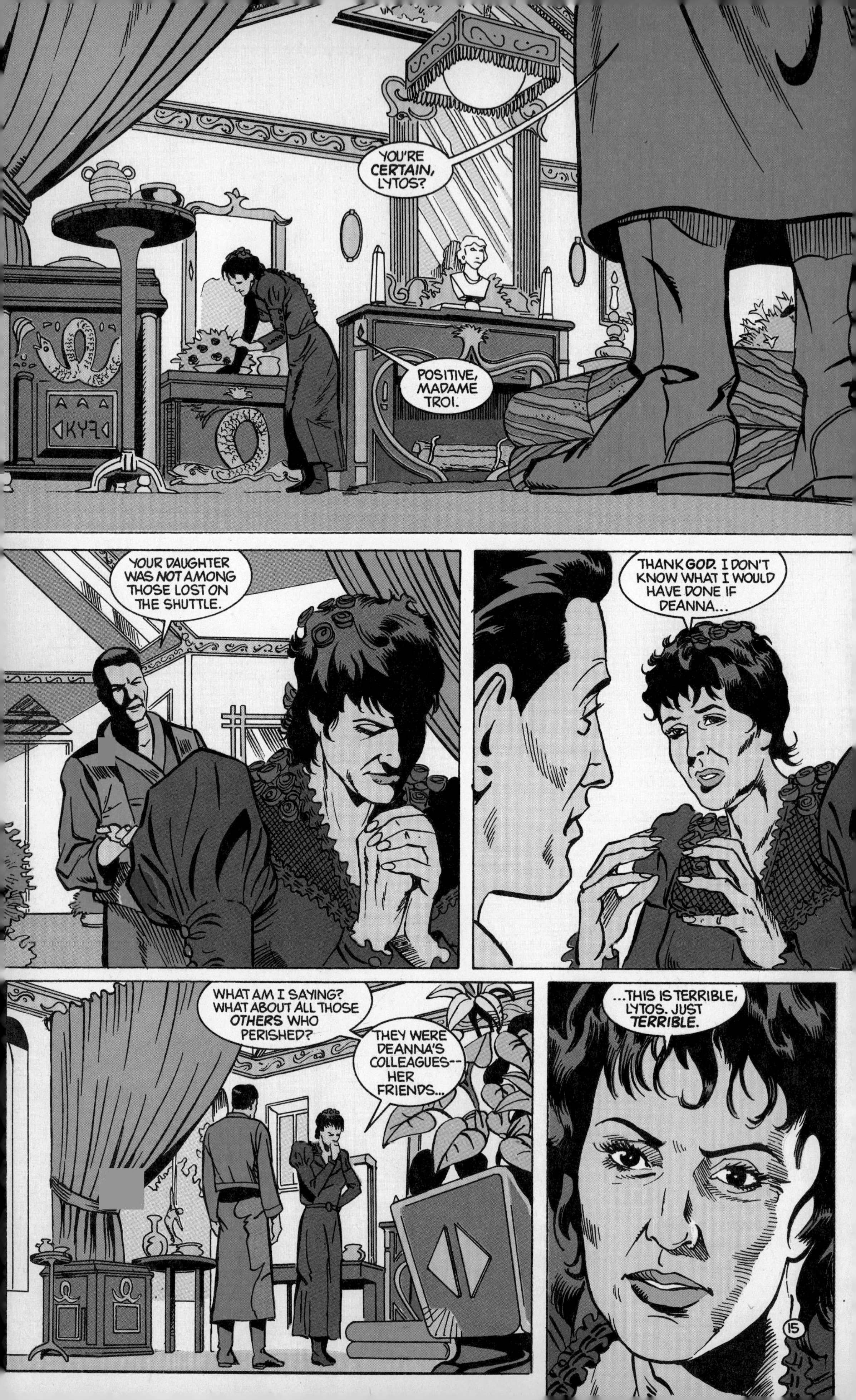

YOU'RE CERTAIN, LYTOS?
POSITIVE, MADAME TROI.

SAY THAT AGAIN, CAPTAIN. AND SAY IT SLOWLY.

THE ENTERPRISE LOST A SHUTTLE, KATE I BELIEVE YOU KNOW SOME OF THOSE ABOARD-- WORKED WITH THEM.

NAMES, CAPTAIN. WHAT ARE THEIR NAMES?

RIKER. CRUSHER-- WESLEY. WORF. SELAR. GOLD. MARINO. FARADAY. NIGATA.

I THOUGHT YOU'D WANT TO KNOW RIGHT AWAY.

YOU THOUGHT RIGHT.
IF YOU'LL EXCUSE ME, I'VE GOT SOME PATIENTS TO SEE...

...THEN I'M GOING TO WANT TO BE ALONE FOR A WHILE. A LONG WHILE.

WELCOME. YOU BRING NEWS OF MY DAUGHTER?
INDEED, SELAK.

BUT IT IS NOT GOOD NEWS.

YOU MUST BE UNCOMFORTABLE STANDING OUT THERE IN THE SUN. PLEASE COME IN.

HEY-- I'VE **GOT** SOMETHING! I'VE GOT A READING!

WHAT **KIND** OF READING?
LIFE, LIEUTENANT! SIGNS OF **LIFE**!

YOU MEAN WE'RE SAVED? WE'VE FOUND A FEDERATION OUTPOST?

UNFORTUNATELY **NOT**, DOCTOR. IT JUST MEANS WE'VE FOUND **LIFE**--OF **SOME** SORT. AND IT'S ADVANCED ENOUGH TO BE OUT IN SPACE.

BUT EVEN IF IT'S **NOT** AN OUTPOST--THEY CAN HELP US, CAN'T THEY? MAYBE THEY CAN REPAIR OUR **STAR**-DRIVE--GIVE US DIRECTIONS BACK HOME!

IT IS NOT THAT SIMPLE.

FOR ONE THING, THESE LIFEFORMS MAY NOT BE ABLE TO SHOW US THE WAY HOME--MUCH LESS TO REPAIR OUR WARP DRIVE. AND EVEN IF THEY CAN DO THESE THINGS, THEY MAY NOT BE INCLINED TO DO SO.

IT IS JUST AS LIKELY THAT THEY WILL WANT TO BLOW US UP.

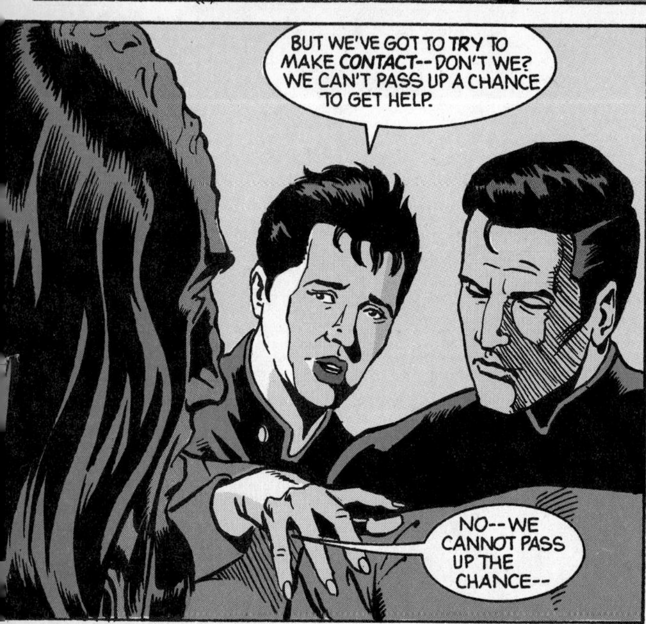
BUT WE'VE GOT TO TRY TO MAKE CONTACT--DON'T WE? WE CAN'T PASS UP A CHANCE TO GET HELP.
NO--WE CANNOT PASS UP THE CHANCE--

"--BUT WE MUST PROCEED WITH CAUTION."
NCC-1701-D
02

ENSIGN CRUSHER--MAINTAIN PRESENT COURSE AND SPEED. BUT BE READY TO RESORT TO EVASIVE MANEUVERS.

AYE, SIR.

I NEVER THOUGHT I'D HEAR THE DAY WHEN A KLINGON CALLED FOR EVASIVE MANEUVERS.

WORF IS NOT JUST ANY KLINGON, DOCTOR. HE IS A STAR-FLEET OFFICER--SWORN TO UPHOLD STARFLEET ETHICS AND PRACTICES.

HIS EMOTIONS MAY BE TELLING HIM NOT TO RUN FROM A FIGHT. BUT HIS TRAINING TELLS HIM OTHERWISE.

AND HIS TRAINING MUST RULE HIS EMOTIONS

IN THE FINAL ANALYSIS, HE MUST ASK HIMSELF WHAT CAPTAIN PICARD WHAT DO--OR WHAT COMMANDER RIKER WOULD DO...

"...OUR SURVIVAL WILL DEPEND ON HOW WELL HE ANSWERS THOSE QUESTIONS."
20

WHY CAN'T I MOURN THEM?
WHY CAN'T I BRING MYSELF TO ACCEPT THEIR DEATHS--AS THE OTHERS HAVE ACCEPTED THEM? AM I JUST BEING FOOLISH? UNREALISTIC?
OR IS IT THAT I NEVER HAD A CHANCE TO TELL THEM HOW I FEEL?
WELL, THAT CAN BE REMEDIED-- AT LEAST, IN A WAY IT CAN.
COMPUTER--ADD TO THIS PROGRAM COMMANDER RIKER, LIEUTENANT WORF AND ENSIGN CRUSHER.
HOW EERIE IT IS TO SEE YOU STANDING HERE BEFORE ME-- JUST AS TASHA YAR ONCE STOOD BEFORE ALL OF US. HOW VERY STRANGE.

WHAT CAN WE DO FOR YOU, SIR?
YOU CAN LISTEN, WILL. SIMPLY LISTEN.
I NEVER TOLD YOU--ANY OF YOU--HOW PROUD I WAS OF YOU. HOW GLAD I WAS TO HAVE YOU WITH ME.
CAPTAINS ARE TOO BUSY TO SAY SUCH THINGS. AND PERHAPS THIS CAPTAIN WAS BUSIER THAN MOST.
BUT I'M TELLING YOU NOW. I RESPECTED YOU. I ADMIRED YOU. AND NOW THAT YOU'RE GONE, I...
22

OH, BLAST! THIS ISN'T WHY I CAN'T MOURN YOU!

IT'S BECAUSE I DON'T BELIEVE YOU'RE DEAD! AND NO AMOUNT OF HOLOGRAPHIC THERAPY IS GOING TO MAKE ME BELIEVE OTHERWISE!

COMPUTER-- TERMINATE PROGRAM.

"WHAT IS IT?"

IT LOOKS LIKE NOT ONE SHIP, BUT MANY.
AS IF THEY WERE ALL MELDED TOGETHER. BUT WHY?

MORE IMPORTANT --CAN IT BE OF HELP TO US? IT EXHIBITS NO EVIDENCE OF PROPULSION CAPABILITIES...

"...TAKE HER IN CLOSER, ENSIGN."
"AYE, SIR."
TO BE CONTINUED...

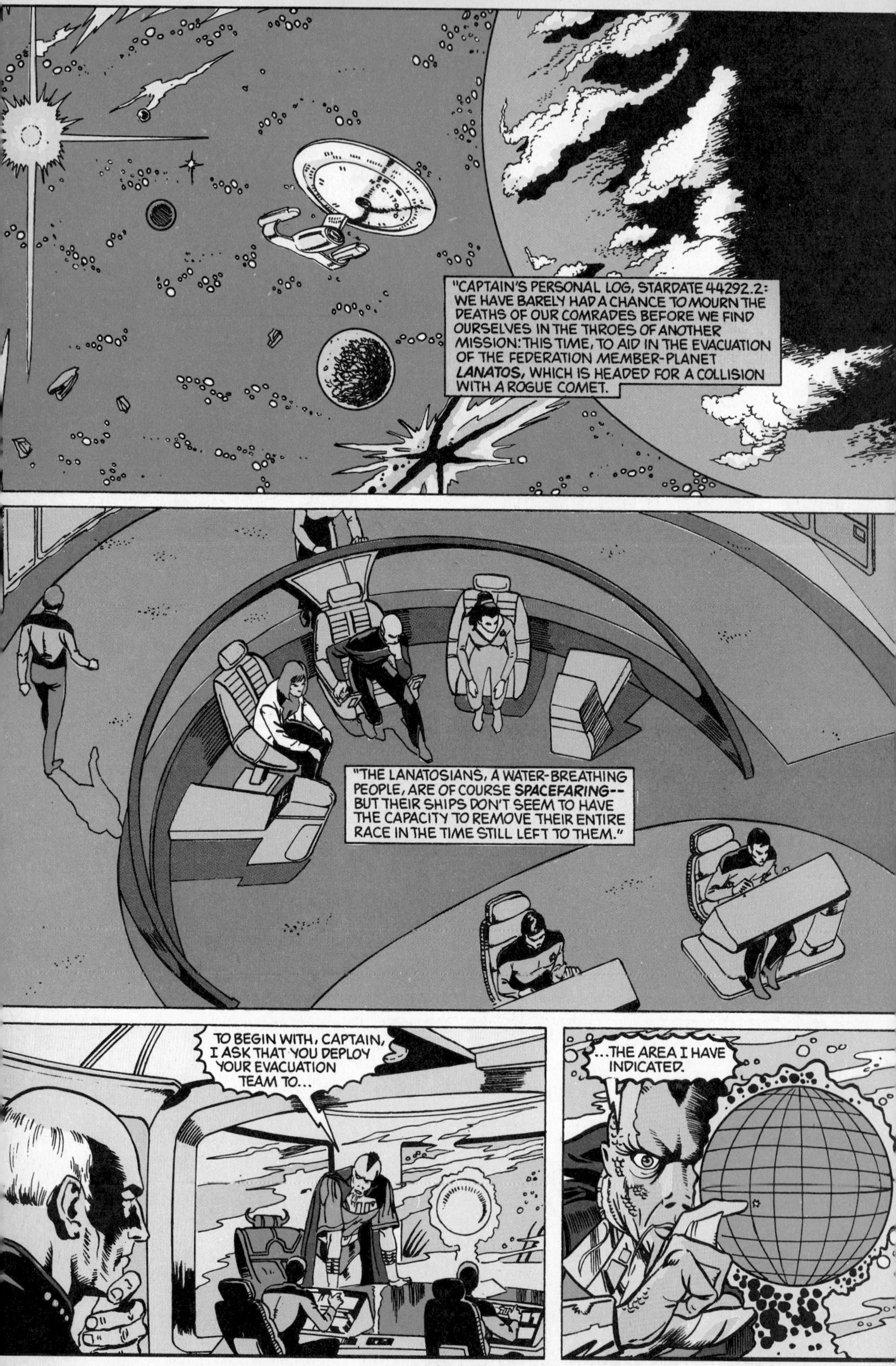

"CAPTAIN'S PERSONAL LOG, STARDATE 44292.2: WE HAVE BARELY HAD A CHANCE TO MOURN THE DEATHS OF OUR COMRADES BEFORE WE FIND OURSELVES IN THE THROES OF ANOTHER MISSION: THIS TIME, TO AID IN THE EVACUATION OF THE FEDERATION MEMBER-PLANET *LANATOS*, WHICH IS HEADED FOR A COLLISION WITH A ROGUE COMET.

I DON'T GET IT, SIR. THE AREA INDICATED BY FIRST GOVERNOR IMLACH IS UNPOPULATED.

PERHAPS THE FIRST GOVERNOR HAS MADE A MISTAKE, SIR?

IT IS NO MISTAKE, CAPTAIN. WHILE THAT AREA IS NOT CURRENTLY POPULATED, IT SERVED AS THE CRADLE OF OUR CIVILIZATION THOUSANDS OF YEARS AGO.

THE MONUMENTS IN THE AREA ARE SACRED TO US. THEY MUST NOT BE LEFT BEHIND.

ARE YOU TELLING ME WE'VE COME ALL THIS WAY... TO RESCUE A COLLECTION OF STONES?

THROUGHOUT HISTORY, CAPTAIN, LANATOSIANS HAVE DIED TO PRESERVE THESE STONES. I DO NOT THINK IT IS ASKING TOO MUCH TO HAVE YOU TRANSPORT THEM.

ANY RESPONSE TO OUR HAIL, ENSIGN?
NONE, SIR. AND I'VE TRIED EVERY FREQUENCY I CAN THINK OF.

"BUT WE KNOW THAT THING IS POPULATED. THE SENSORS ARE PICKING UP ALL KINDS OF LIFE SIGNS."

WHICH MEANS ONE OF TWO THINGS--EITHER THEY CAN'T COMMUNICATE, OR THEY JUST WON'T.

STILL, IT WOULD SEEM UNWISE TO BYPASS IT--WHEN IT COULD OFFER US A WAY OF GETTING HOME.
TRUE, DOCTOR. BUT IT COULD ALSO OFFER US A VIOLENT DEATH, IF ITS WEAPONRY IS STILL INTACT.

IF IT WAS GOING TO ATTACK US, IT WOULD HAVE DONE SO ALREADY. I SAY WE TRY TO BOARD IT!

THAT IS MY DECISION, DOCTOR. MINE AND MINE ALONE.

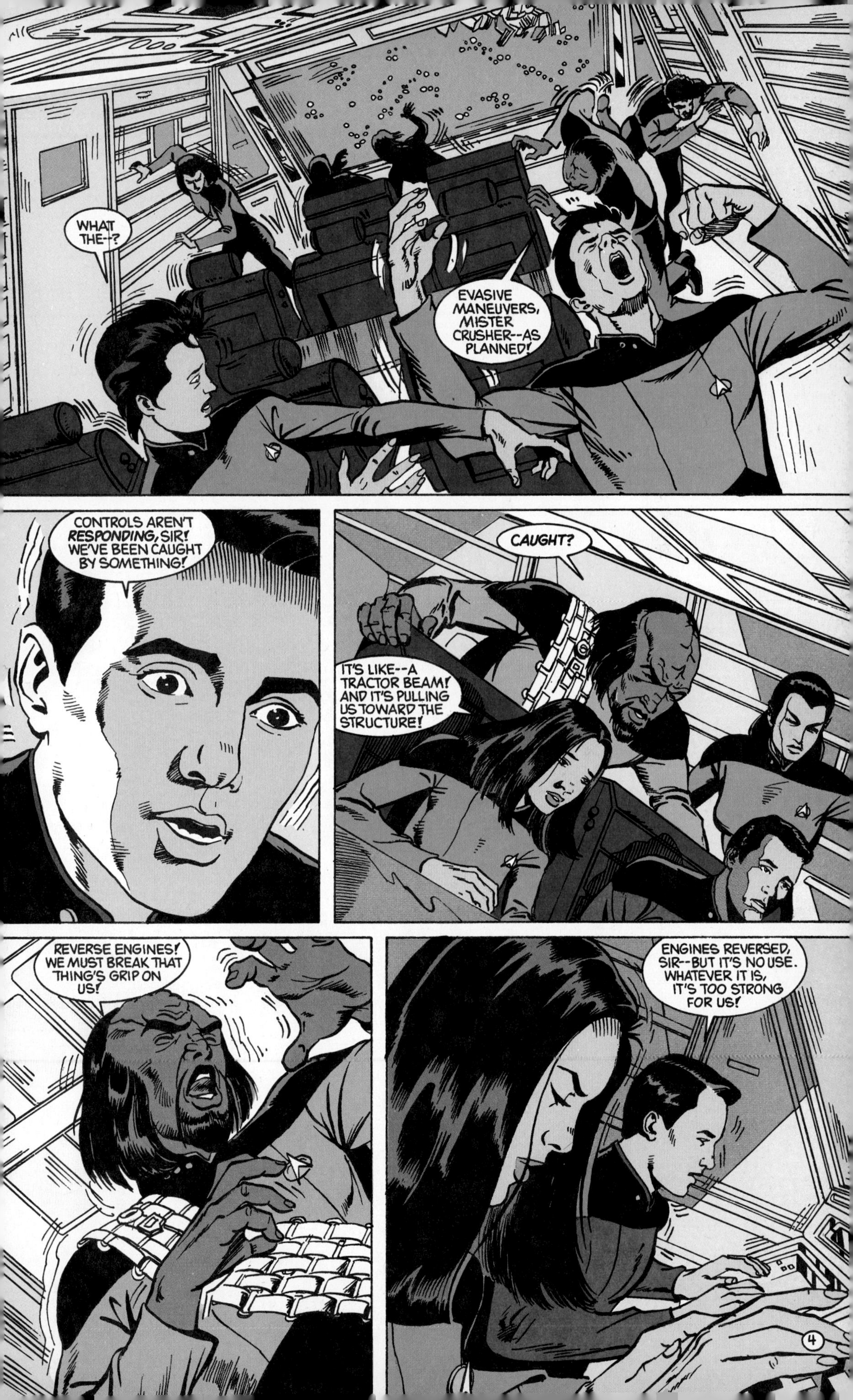

WHAT THE--?
EVASIVE MANEUVERS, MISTER CRUSHER--AS PLANNED!

"PERHAPS WE'VE LOST THIS BATTLE--BUT WE WILL WIN THE *WAR*, MISTER CRUSHER. ENGINES IN NEUTRAL.

"ENSIGN NIGATA--DISTRIBUTE PHASERS. WHOEVER HAS SNARED US MAY FIND HE'S GOTTEN *MORE* THAN HE BARGAINED FOR."

TRAPPED

MICHAEL JAN FRIEDMAN
WRITER
PETER KRAUSE
PENCILLER
PABLO MARCOS
INKER
BOB PINAHA
LETTERER
JULIANNA FERRITER
COLORIST
ROBERT GREENBERGER
EDITOR

BASED ON STAR TREK: THE NEXT GENERATION CREATED BY GENE RODDENBERRY

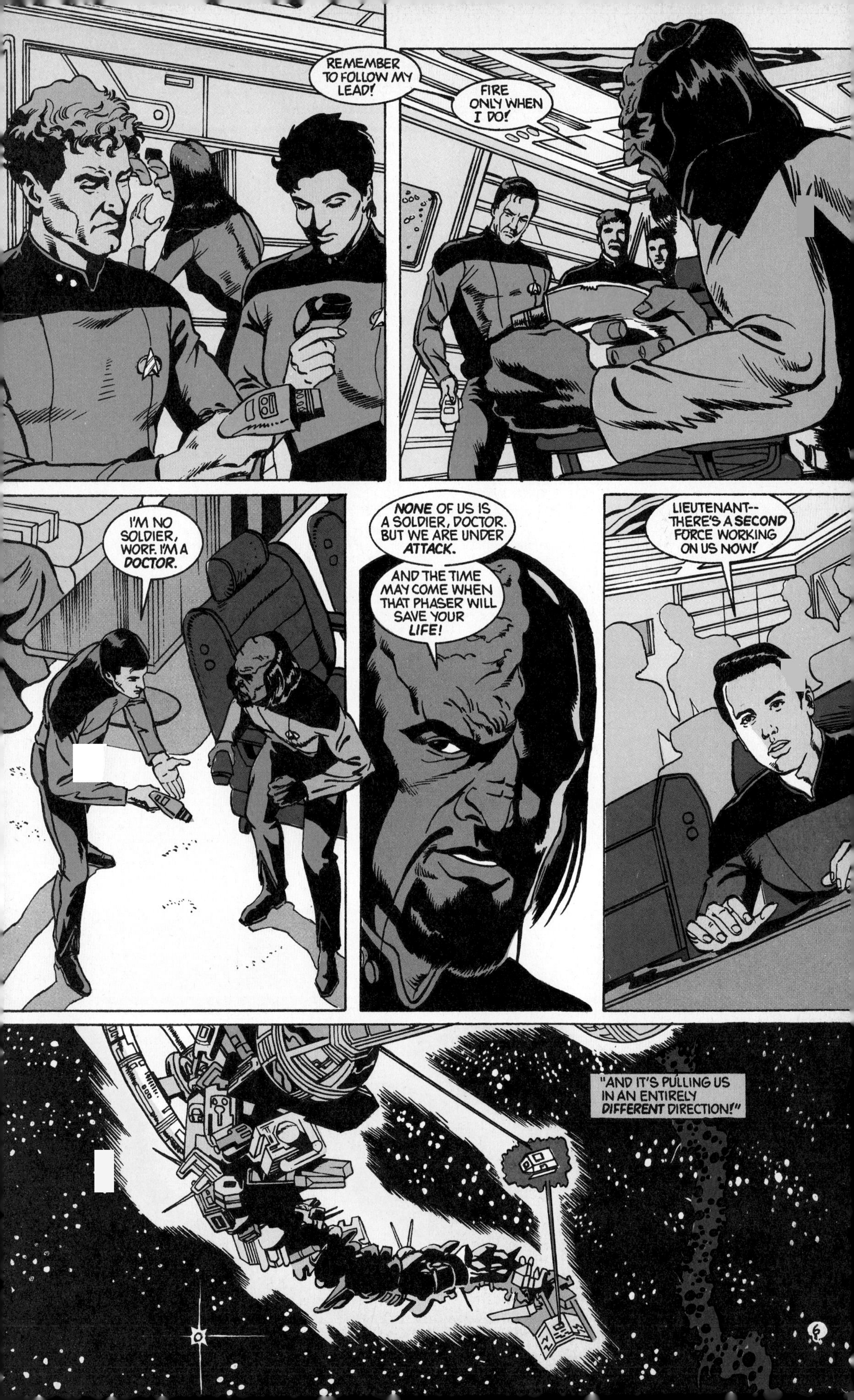

REMEMBER TO FOLLOW MY LEAD!

FIRE ONLY WHEN I DO!

I'M NO SOLDIER, WORF. I'M A **DOCTOR**.

NONE OF US IS A SOLDIER, DOCTOR. BUT WE ARE UNDER ***ATTACK***.

AND THE TIME MAY COME WHEN THAT PHASER WILL SAVE YOUR ***LIFE***!

LIEUTENANT-- THERE'S A **SECOND** FORCE WORKING ON US NOW!

"HOW'S IT GOING DOWN THERE, DATA?"
NCC-1701-D
ALL IS PROCEEDING ACCORDING TO SCHEDULE, GEORDI.
WE HAVE BEGUN THE DISMANTLING PROCESS. YOU SHOULD BE ABLE TO START BEAMING UP THE FIRST PIECES IN LESS THAN AN HOUR.
TERRIFIC. AND THANKS FOR YOUR HELP, DATA.
I WISH I COULD'VE BEEN DOWN THERE MYSELF--BUT THE PREPARATION OF THESE MARINE ENVIRONMENT TANKS IS TAKING UP ALL MY TIME. AND SINCE I CAN'T BE IN TWO PLACES AT ONCE...

...WELL, LIKE I SAY-- I APPRECIATE IT.
IT IS NO TROUBLE AT ALL. IN FACT, I FIND THE ASSIGNMENT *QUITE* ENGAGING-- FROM A SOCIOLOGICAL VIEWPOINT.

DAMN!
STATUS REPORT, ENSIGN!
IT SEEMS TO BE A STALEMATE FOR THE MOMENT--BOTH BEAMS ARE EXERTING EQUAL FORCE!
WAIT--THE FIRST BEAM IS LOSING POWER! IT'S FADING!
SOMETHING'S CHANGING IN THE STRUCTURE'S SURFACE, SIR. THERE'S AN OPENING THAT WASN'T THERE BEFORE.
"WE'RE IN THE GRIP OF THE SECOND BEAM ALONE. IT'S PULLING US TOWARD THE OTHER END OF THE STRUCTURE."
9

"IT LOOKS LIKE AN AIRLOCK OF SOME KIND. AND IT'S ADJUSTING TO FIT THE SIZE OF OUR CRAFT."

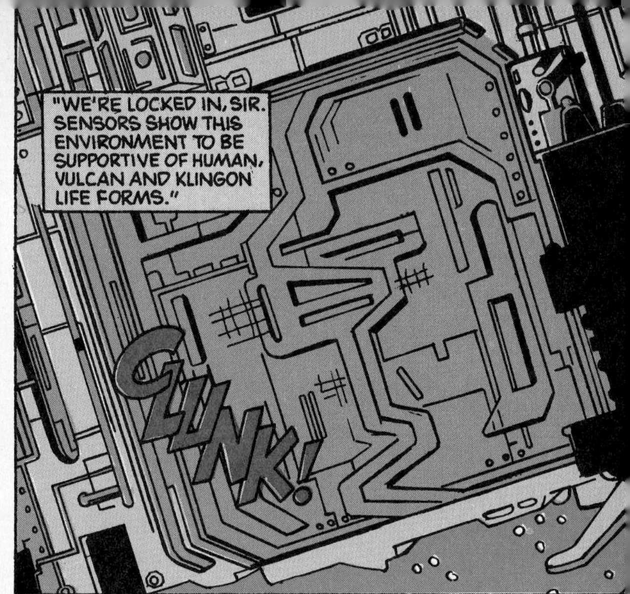
"WE'RE LOCKED IN, SIR. SENSORS SHOW THIS ENVIRONMENT TO BE SUPPORTIVE OF HUMAN, VULCAN AND KLINGON LIFE FORMS."
CLUNK!

NOW WHAT?

THERE IS NO POINT IN SITTING HERE, PRISONERS IN OUR OWN VESSEL. LET US SEE WHO HAS TAKEN US PRISONER--AND WHY.

OPEN THE DOOR, MISTER CRUSHER.

WELCOME.

I CANNOT BE SURE, SIR, BUT I THINK THE LANATOSIANS ARE HOLDING SOMETHING BACK.
YOU MEAN DECEIVING US, COUNSELOR?

I HESITATE TO USE SO STRONG A WORD--PARTICULARLY SINCE THEIR EMOTIONS ARE NOT AS CLEAR TO ME AS THOSE OF OTHER RACES. ON THE OTHER HAND, I WOULD NOT RULE IT OUT.
BUT WHAT HAVE THEY GOT TO HIDE?

THAT IS WHAT I HOPE TO FIND OUT, CAPTAIN. BY VISITING THE PLANET MYSELF. AND SEEING THE DISMANTLING SITE FIRSTHAND.

YOU BELIEVE THIS HAS SOMETHING TO DO WITH THE MONUMENTS?
IT IS JUST A GUESS, SIR. BUT AN EDUCATED ONE.

PICARD TO TRANSPORTER ROOM ONE. MISTER O'BRIEN--I WOULD APPRECIATE IT IF YOU WOULD BEAM DOWN COUNSELOR TROI--AT HER EARLIEST CONVENIENCE, OF COURSE.
BE GLAD TO, CAPTAIN.

I WILL GET READY, SIR.
VERY WELL. AND PERHAPS WE CAN DO AWAY WITH THE COUNSELOR TITLE FOR THE TIME BEING. IT WILL ONLY PUT THE LANATOSIANS ON THEIR GUARD.

IF ANYONE ASKS, YOU ARE LIEUTENANT COMMANDER TROI--HARDLY A LIE, THOUGH WE DON'T OFTEN REFER TO YOU THAT WAY.

AND YOU HAVE BEEN ASSIGNED TO THIS OPERATION SIMPLY BECAUSE YOU'RE ONE OF MY **BEST** OFFICERS-- NO OTHER REASON. UNDERSTOOD?
UNDERSTOOD, CAPTAIN.

BEFORE I GO, HOWEVER, THERE IS SOMETHING THAT MUST BE DISCUSSED.
WHAT IS THAT, COUNSELOR?

IT IS TIME YOU FOUND **REPLACEMENTS** FOR COMMANDER RIKER AND LIEUTENANT WORF, SIR.
YOU HAVE YET TO FILL THEIR SPOTS IN THE COMMAND STRUCTURE.

I ***AM AWARE*** OF IT, DEANNA. IT IS JUST THAT I CANNOT BRING MYSELF TO BELIEVE THEY ARE GONE. SOMETHING INSIDE ME KEEPS SAYING OTHERWISE.
NONETHELESS, I RECOGNIZE MY DUTY IN THIS REGARD. AS SOON AS MISTER DATA RETURNS FROM LANATOS, I WILL NAME HIM FIRST OFFICER-- DESPITE THE FACT THAT GOOD PEOPLE SUCH AS COMMANDER SHELBY ARE WAITING IN THE WINGS...

"...AND THE POSITION OF ACTING SECURITY CHIEF WILL BE TURNED OVER TO MISTER BURKE. I WANT TO CONSULT WITH STARFLEET ON THE BEST PERSON QUALIFIED..."

...NOW GET GOING, COUNSELOR--I MEAN, ***COMMANDER.***
AYE, SIR.
12

WHO ARE YOU?
MY NAME IS DARIOS APPOLENE-- A BETAZOID, AS YOU CAN SEE.
THOUGH I SENSE THAT YOU FEAR US, DISTRUST US...THERE IS NO REASON TO DO SO. WE ARE YOUR FRIENDS.
020
NCC-1701-D
02
THEN WHY DID YOU BRING US HERE AGAINST OUR WILL?
THERE WAS NO OTHER WAY--AS YOU WILL SEE.
PLEASE-- FOLLOW ME AND ALL WILL BE EXPLAINED.
AND BRING YOUR WOUNDED COMRADE. WE HAVE MEDICAL FACILITIES HERE WHICH MAY BE OF USE TO HIM.

WE ARE GLAD YOU HAVE COME TO UNDERSTAND THE IMPORTANCE OF THESE MONUMENTS, COMMANDER. AFTER ALL, THEY ARE THE FOCAL POINT OF MY PEOPLE'S CULTURAL AND RELIGIOUS TRADITION.
SURELY YOUR PEOPLE HAVE SUCH PRIZED POSSESSIONS-- DO THEY NOT?
PERHAPS WE DO, THIRD GOVERNOR EZRECH. I HAVE NEVER GIVEN IT MUCH THOUGHT.
THE FACT OF THE MATTER IS TELEPATHIC CULTURES SELDOM HAVE NEED OF SUCH TANGIBLE SYMBOLS.
BUT I CANNOT COME OUT AND SAY THAT. IT IS IMPORTANT THAT NO ONE HERE KNOW OF MY TALENTS.
ESPECIALLY SINCE I'M GETTING THE SAME FEELINGS OF DUPLICITY FROM EZRECH AS I GOT FROM IMLACH.
WAIT--I FELT SOMETHING! AND IT IS NOT COMING FROM EZRECH!
IT IS DISTANT-- YET POWERFUL!

I MUST FOLLOW IT TO ITS SOURCE!
YOU MUST EXCUSE ME, THIRD GOVERNOR. I HAVE WORK TO DO.
OF COURSE, COMMANDER TROI.

I HOPE NO ONE WILL NOTICE IF I SLIP AWAY... MUST FOCUS ON THE FEELING BEFORE IT CAN FADE...

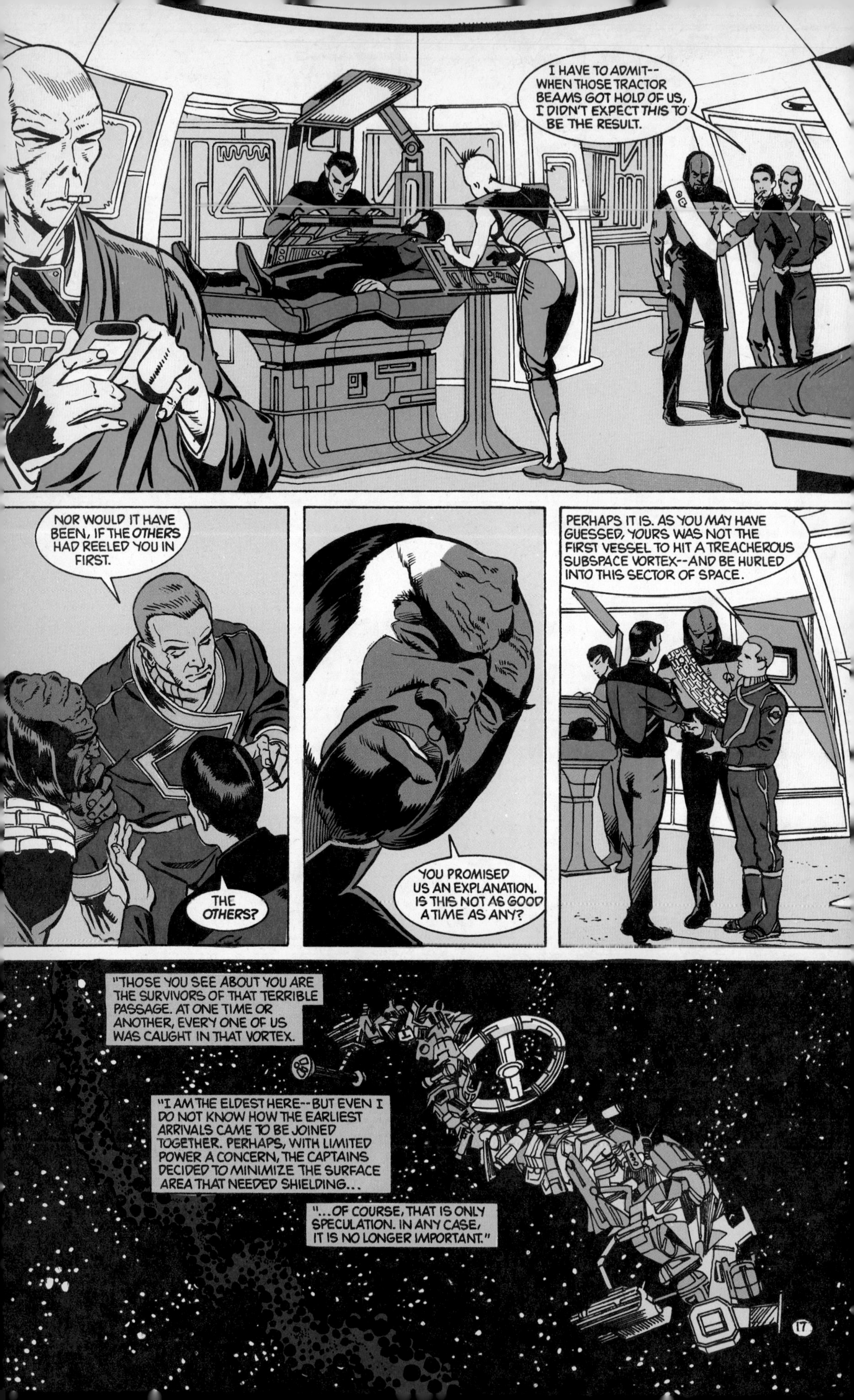

I HAVE TO ADMIT--WHEN THOSE TRACTOR BEAMS GOT HOLD OF US, I DIDN'T EXPECT *THIS* TO BE THE RESULT.

WHAT IS IMPORTANT IS THAT NOT EVERYONE HERE WOULD HAVE GREETED YOU AS WE DID. YOU SEE, ONLY HALF OF THIS STRUCTURE IS OCCUPIED BY RACES FRIENDLY TO THE FEDERATION...
"...ANDORIANS, FOR INSTANCE, AS WELL AS TELLARITES, BENZITES AND SO ON."
THE OTHER HALF IS THE STRONGHOLD OF RACES HOSTILE TO THE FEDERATION. ROMULANS. FERENGI. AND, OF COURSE, KLINGONS.
I HAVE ALREADY SEARCHED YOUR MIND, WORF. I KNOW THAT THE KLINGON EMPIRE HAS ESTABLISHED A DIFFERENT SORT OF RELATIONSHIP WITH THE FEDERATION IN THE PRESENT DAY...
"...BUT THE KLINGONS OF WHICH I SPEAK ARRIVED HERE BEFORE THE ALLIANCE WAS MADE. AS FAR AS THEY ARE CONCERNED, THE FEDERATION IS THEIR ENEMY--"
--AND THAT WOULD INCLUDE A KLINGON IN A STARFLEET UNIFORM. HAD THEY WON THE CONTEST OF TRACTOR BEAMS, WORF, YOU WOULD HAVE DIED, I ASSURE YOU.
18

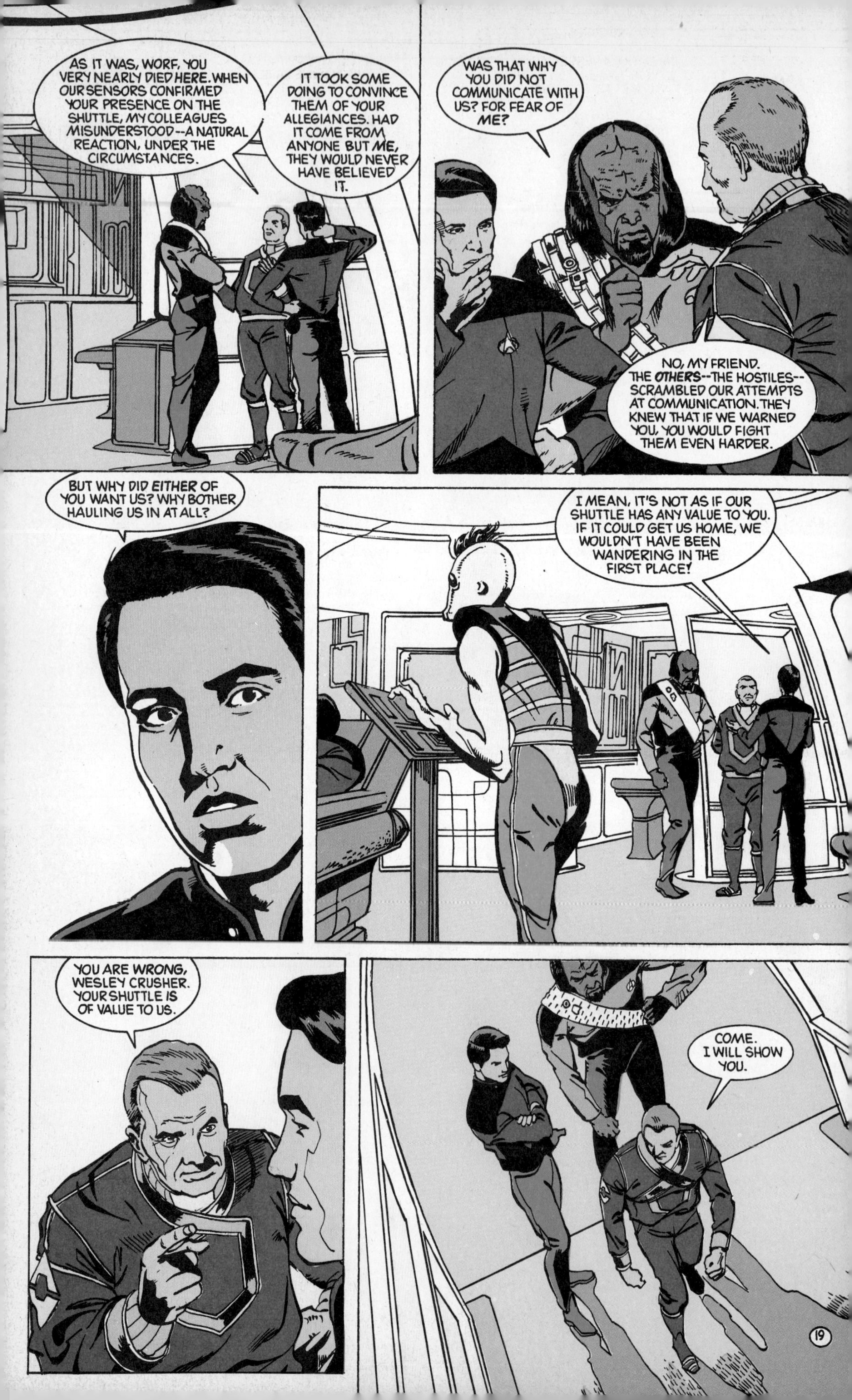

AS IT WAS, WORF, YOU VERY NEARLY DIED HERE. WHEN OUR SENSORS CONFIRMED YOUR PRESENCE ON THE SHUTTLE, MY COLLEAGUES MISUNDERSTOOD--A NATURAL REACTION, UNDER THE CIRCUMSTANCES.

IT TOOK SOME DOING TO CONVINCE THEM OF YOUR ALLEGIANCES. HAD IT COME FROM ANYONE BUT *ME*, THEY WOULD NEVER HAVE BELIEVED IT.

WAS THAT WHY YOU DID NOT COMMUNICATE WITH US? FOR FEAR OF *ME*?

NO, MY FRIEND. THE *OTHERS*--THE HOSTILES--SCRAMBLED OUR ATTEMPTS AT COMMUNICATION. THEY KNEW THAT IF WE WARNED YOU, YOU WOULD FIGHT THEM EVEN HARDER.

BUT WHY DID *EITHER* OF YOU WANT US? WHY BOTHER HAULING US IN AT ALL?

I MEAN, IT'S NOT AS IF OUR SHUTTLE HAS ANY VALUE TO YOU. IF IT COULD GET US HOME, WE WOULDN'T HAVE BEEN WANDERING IN THE FIRST PLACE!

NOT LONG AGO, A VESSEL OF UNKNOWN ORIGIN WAS SPEWED OUT OF SUBSPACE JUST AS YOU WERE. BUT UNLIKE YOU, THE OCCUPANTS DID NOT SURVIVE THE JOURNEY--OUR SENSORS WERE VERY CLEAR ABOUT THAT.
HOWEVER, THE SHIP'S WARP DRIVE FARED BETTER. AS FAR AS WE CAN TELL, IT IS INTACT. COMPLETELY FUNCTIONAL.
THEN THIS SHIP OFFERS US ALL A WAY HOME!
INDEED IT DOES. HOWEVER, OUR TRACTOR BEAMS ARE NOT POWERFUL ENOUGH TO BRING IT TO US.
THEREFORE, WE MUST GET TO IT. AND THAT IS THE VALUE OF YOUR SHUTTLE!

...CAN'T LOSE THE THREAD...IT IS FAINT NOW, SO FAINT...

...MUST BE KILOMETERS FROM THE WORK SITE... BUT I CANNOT QUIT NOW...

MY GOD!

...MEAN YOU... NO HARM...NEED HELP...

...IT IS MORE THAN JUST SENTIENT. IT HAS AN INTELLECT!

AND ALSO THE ABILITY TO COMMUNICATE TELEPATHICALLY--LIKE A FULL-BLOODED BETAZOID!

...IMPRISONED... MUST ESCAPE...

...BUT THE WALL PREVENTS...
THIS CREATURE HAS BEEN TRAPPED HERE--BEHIND THAT WALL! I THOUGHT IT LOOKED ARTIFICIAL!
BUT WHO WOULD DO SUCH A THING? AND WHY?

YOU SHOULD NOT HAVE COME HERE. NOW YOU KNOW TOO MUCH...

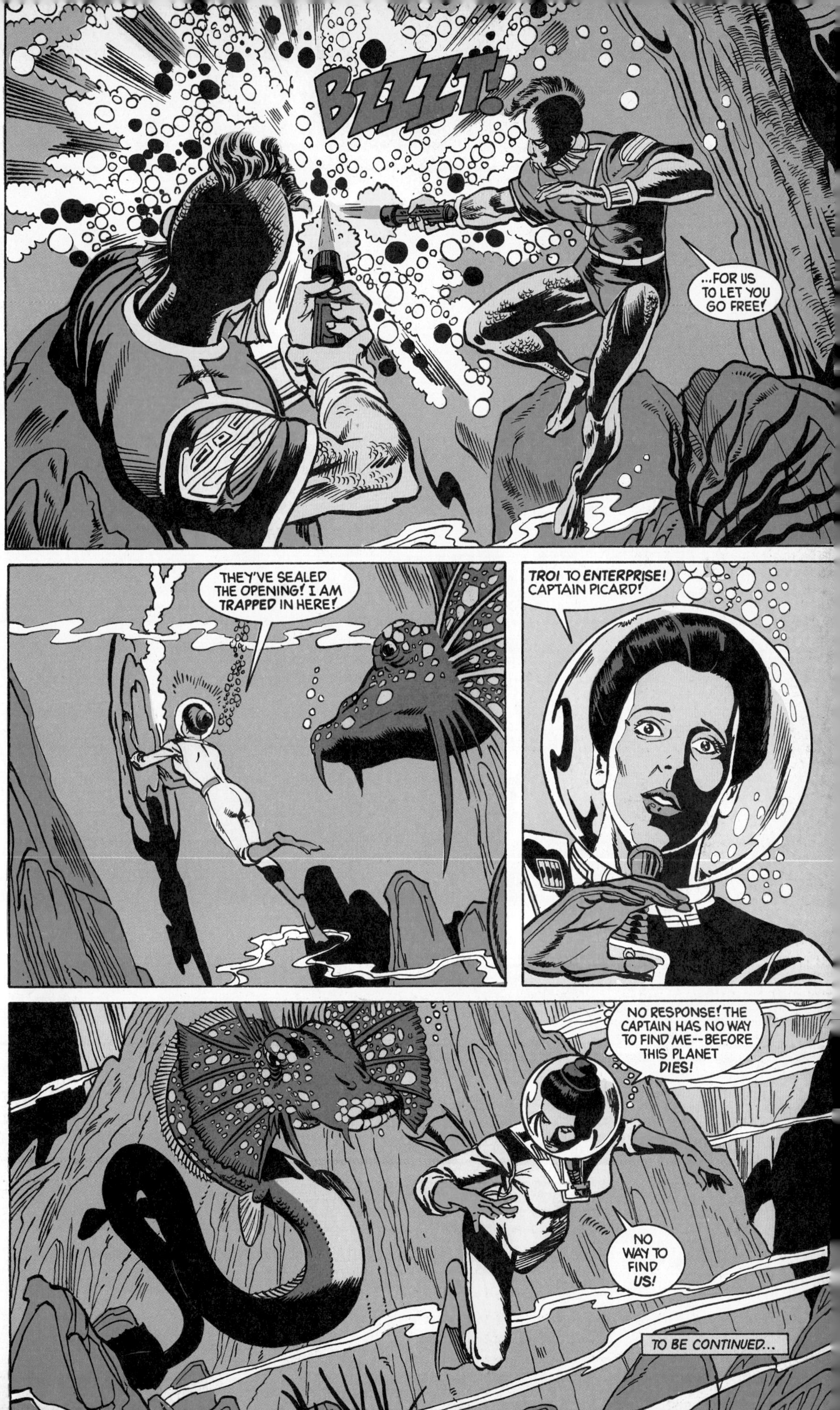

BZZZT!
...FOR US TO LET YOU GO FREE!

CAPTAIN? CAPTAIN PICARD?
WHAT IS IT, MISTER LAFORGE?
IT'S COUNSELOR TROI, SIR. WE CAN'T FIND HER.
CAN'T FIND HER?
NO, SIR. WE LOST HER SIGNAL A FEW MOMENTS AGO. AND WHEN WE TRIED TO CONTACT HER, THERE WAS NO RESPONSE.
I--EXCUSE ME, SIR. THERE'S A COMMUNICATION COMING THROUGH FROM FIRST GOVERNOR IMLACH.
PUT IT ON THE SCREEN, MISTER BELIX.
WHERE IS CAPTAIN PICARD? I HAVE SERIOUS MATTERS TO DISCUSS WITH HIM.
HE'S UNAVAILABLE RIGHT NOW, FIRST GOVERNOR. CAN I HELP YOU?
THE WORK ON THE MONUMENTS IS NOT PROCEEDING SWIFTLY ENOUGH. YOU MUST DEPLOY MORE MANPOWER TO THE SITE.

EVERYTHING IS GOING ACCORDING TO SCHEDULE, FIRST GOVERNOR. WE'VE STILL GOT A COUPLE OF DAYS BEFORE THE COMET HITS.

OBVIOUSLY, COMMANDER, YOU DO NOT UNDERSTAND THE IMPORTANCE OF THOSE MONUMENTS. THEY ARE THE *LIFEBLOOD* OF OUR PEOPLE. WITHOUT THEM--
I GET THE IDEA, FIRST GOVERNOR. WE'LL SEE WHAT WE CAN DO TO EXPEDITE THE PROCESS.
SEE TO IT *QUICKLY*, COMMANDER. TIME IS OF THE ESSENCE!

I TAKE IT YOU HEARD THAT, CAPTAIN?
INDEED I DID.

HOW IS THE EVACUATION OF THE FIRST GOVERNOR'S *PEOPLE* GOING?
FINE, SIR. COULDN'T BE BETTER.

THEN HIS *MONUMENTS* BE ***DAMNED***. I'VE GOT A MISSING OFFICER ON MY HANDS!

AND THAT'S MY FIRST PRIORITY!

AYE, CAPTAIN?
SOMETHING HAS HAPPENED TO COUNSELOR TROI, DATA. WE'VE LOST HER SIGNAL.
I HAVE NOT SEEN HER FOR SOME TIME, SIR. I HAVE BEEN DEVOTING MY ATTENTION TO THE DISMANTLING OF THE MONUMENTS.
I UNDERSTAND. BUT I'M GIVING YOU A NEW ASSIGNMENT--FIND COUNSELOR TROI.
CERTAINLY, SIR. DO YOU HAVE ANY SUGGESTIONS AS TO HOW?
I WISH I DID, COMMANDER. BUT I DO NOT. I AM AFRAID YOU WILL HAVE TO SOLVE THIS PROBLEM ON YOUR OWN.
PICARD OUT.
I'VE ALREADY LOST THE CREW OF THE EINSTEIN. I'M NOT ABOUT TO LOSE DEANNA AS WELL!

THE BARRIER
IT IS WORSE THAN I THOUGHT. THERE IS NOT JUST ONE CREATURE TRAPPED HERE--
--THERE IS AN ENTIRE HERD!
MICHAEL JAN FRIEDMAN WRITER PETER KRAUSE PENCILLER PABLO MARCOS INKER
BOB PINAHA LETTERER JULIANNA FERRITER COLORIST ROBERT GREENBERGER EDITOR
BASED ON STAR TREK: THE NEXT GENERATION CREATED BY GENE RODDENBERRY
4

WE ARE PEACEFUL... BUT BUILDER-CREATURES THINK US DANGEROUS... LOATHSOME...
BUILDER-CREATURES--THAT MUST MEAN THE LANATOSIANS!
HUNTED BY BUILDER-CREATURES... KILLED... WE ARE ALL THAT IS LEFT...
...WHEN SKYSHIP COMING... BUILDER-CREATURES HERDED US... BUILT WALL TO IMPRISON US...
...TO CONCEAL US...KEEP US SECRET FROM SKYSHIP CREATURES...
...IF SKYSHIP CREATURES KNOW OF US...TAKE US INTO SKY INSTEAD OF STONES...

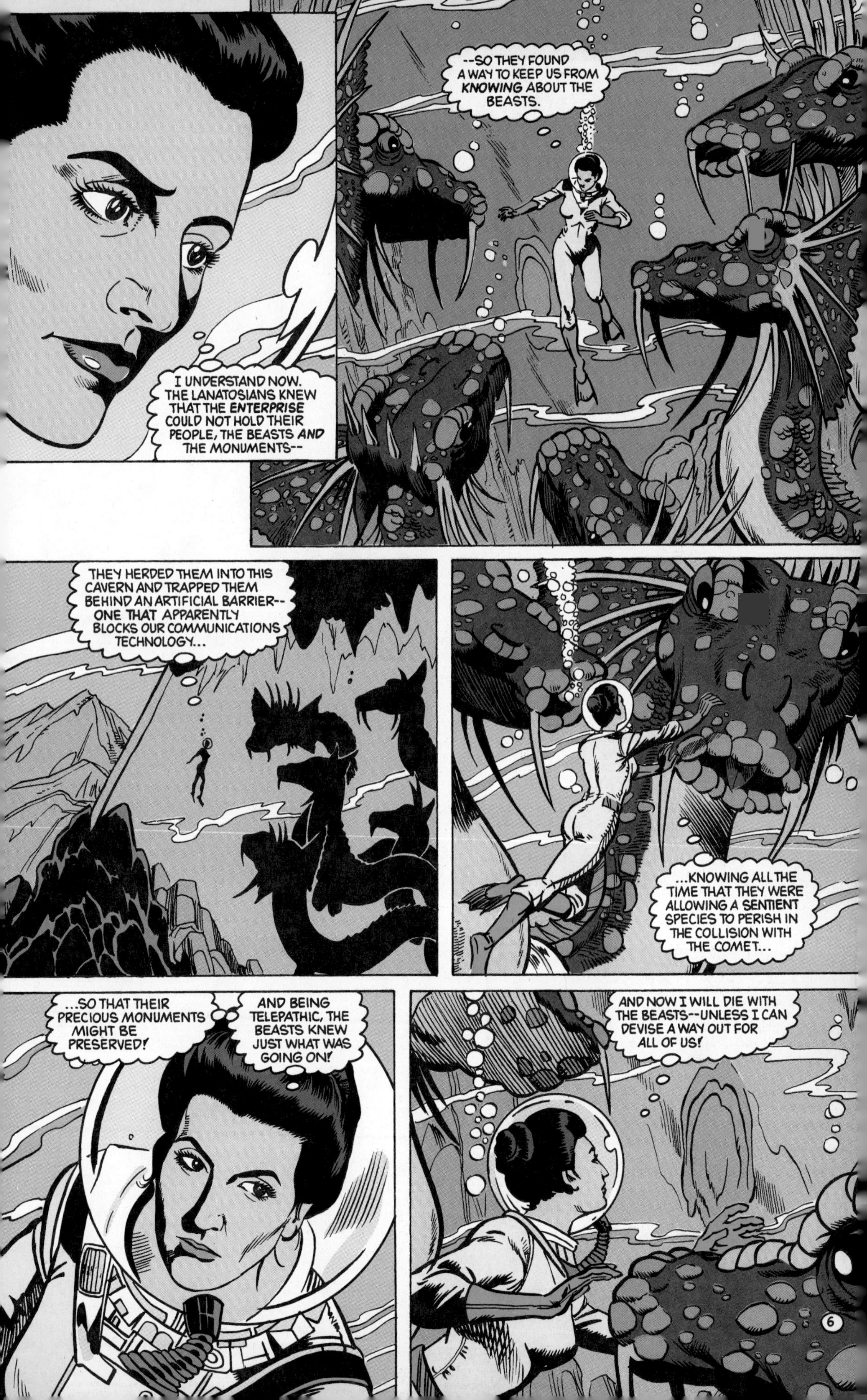

I UNDERSTAND NOW. THE LANATOSIANS KNEW THAT THE ***ENTERPRISE*** COULD NOT HOLD THEIR PEOPLE, THE BEASTS ***AND*** THE MONUMENTS--

--SO THEY FOUND A WAY TO KEEP US FROM ***KNOWING*** ABOUT THE BEASTS.

SO YOU SEE, THAT SHIP CAN NO LONGER HELP ITS ORIGINAL OCCUPANTS-- BUT THAT DOES NOT MEAN IT CANNOT HELP *US*.
AND NOW THERE IS A WAY TO REACH IT-- THROUGH THE USE OF OUR SHUTTLE.
COULDN'T YOU HAVE SEPARATED A VESSEL FROM THE REST OF THE STRUCTURE--AND REACHED THE SHIP *THAT* WAY?
I AM AFRAID NOT. OUR VESSELS HAVE LONG SINCE LOST THEIR INDEPENDENT DRIVE CAPABILITIES. WERE IT NOT FOR THEIR INTEGRATION INTO THE STRUCTURE, THEY WOULD BE NOTHING MORE THAN SPACE DEBRIS.
AND AS I HAVE ALREADY MENTIONED, OUR TRACTOR BEAMS ARE NOT POWERFUL ENOUGH TO DRAW THE SHIP TO US.
FORTUNATELY, *THEY* WERE POWERFUL ENOUGH TO DRAW *YOUR* CRAFT-- BEFORE THE *OTHERS* COULD GET TO YOU.
7

CAN YOU IMAGINE WHAT THIS MEANS TO US, WORF? FOR THE FIRST TIME IN MANY YEARS, WE HAVE HOPE...
"...JUST AS WE HAVE GIVEN YOU HOPE THAT YOUR COMRADE WILL SURVIVE HIS INJURIES."
"WE BELIEVED WE WOULD END OUR DAYS ON THIS JUMBLE OF USELESS SHIPS--LIKE OUR PREDECESSORS HERE. FOR US, THIS IS NOTHING SHORT OF A MIRACLE."
WHAT IS MORE, THAT SHIP IS BIG ENOUGH TO TAKE ALL OF US WHO DWELL ON THIS SIDE OF THE STRUCTURE. ANDORIANS, BENZITES, VULCANS, TELLARITES... NONE NEED BE LEFT BEHIND.
THERE IS ONLY ONE PROBLEM. EVEN IF WE REACH THE SHIP... EVEN IF ITS PROPULSION CAPABILITIES ARE INTACT...
...WE STILL DO NOT KNOW WHERE WE ARE. WE STILL DO NOT KNOW WHICH DIRECTION IS HOME.

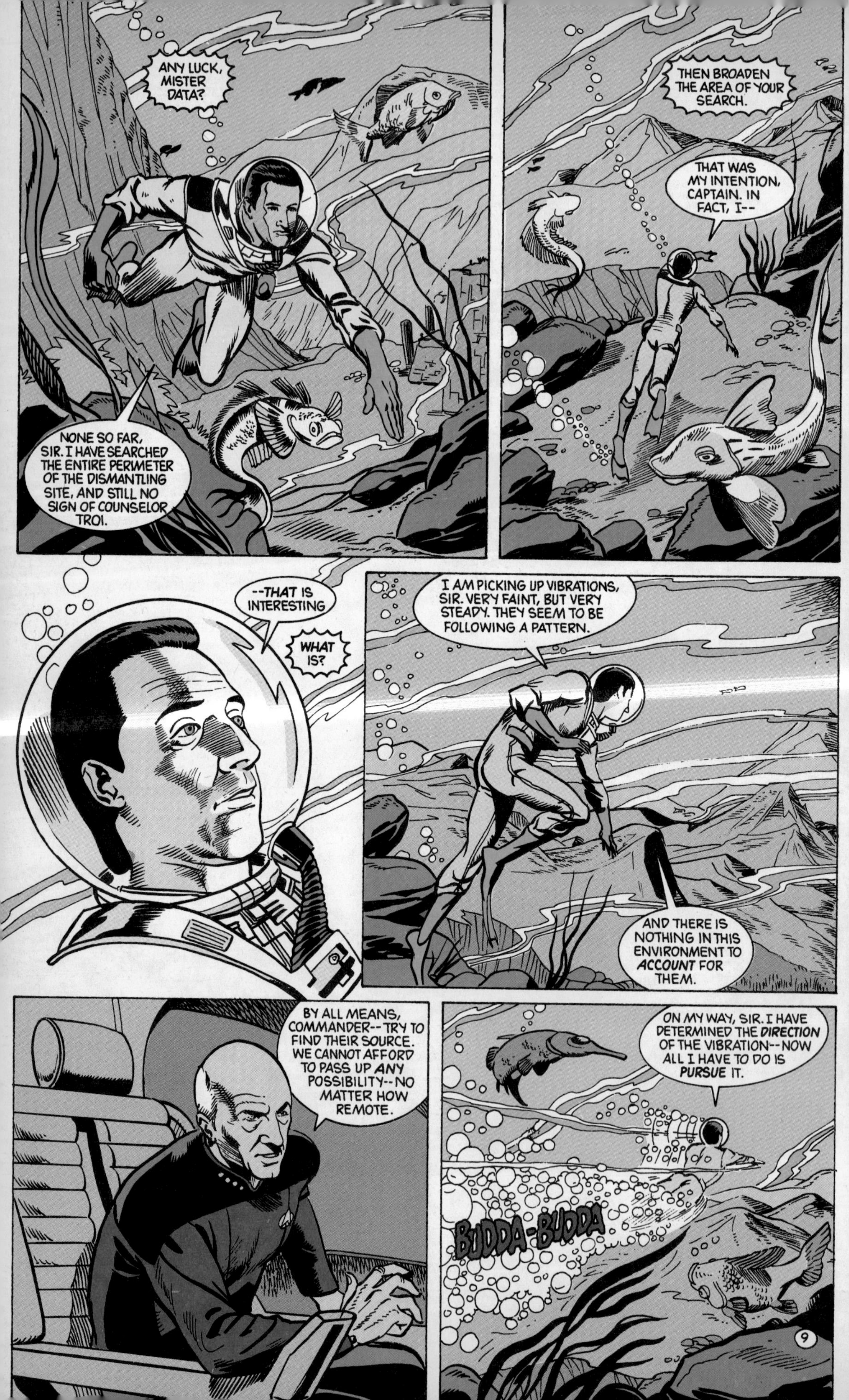
ANY LUCK, MISTER DATA?
NONE SO FAR, SIR. I HAVE SEARCHED THE ENTIRE PERIMETER OF THE DISMANTLING SITE, AND STILL NO SIGN OF COUNSELOR TROI.
THEN BROADEN THE AREA OF YOUR SEARCH.
THAT WAS MY INTENTION, CAPTAIN. IN FACT, I--
--THAT IS INTERESTING
WHAT IS?
I AM PICKING UP VIBRATIONS, SIR. VERY FAINT, BUT VERY STEADY. THEY SEEM TO BE FOLLOWING A PATTERN.
AND THERE IS NOTHING IN THIS ENVIRONMENT TO ACCOUNT FOR THEM.
BY ALL MEANS, COMMANDER-- TRY TO FIND THEIR SOURCE. WE CANNOT AFFORD TO PASS UP ANY POSSIBILITY--NO MATTER HOW REMOTE.
ON MY WAY, SIR. I HAVE DETERMINED THE DIRECTION OF THE VIBRATION--NOW ALL I HAVE TO DO IS PURSUE IT.
BUDDA-BUDDA
9

CAPTAIN! WHAT IS THE MEANING OF THIS?
THE MEANING OF WHAT, FIRST GOVERNOR?
I ASKED YOU TO DEPLOY MORE PERSONNEL--NOT FEWER! I HAVE JUST REVIEWED A REPORT THAT COMMANDERS TROI AND DATA HAVE BOTH LEFT THE MONUMENT AREA!
THAT IS CORRECT, FIRST GOVERNOR. COMMANDER TROI HAS MYSTERIOUSLY DISAPPEARED--AND COMMANDER DATA HAS BEEN DISPATCHED TO FIND HER.
THIS IS INEXCUSABLE, CAPTAIN! OUR MOST PRECIOUS POSSESSIONS ARE IN JEOPARDY--AND YOUR PEOPLE ARE WASTING TIME LOOKING FOR ONE ANOTHER!
THE FEDERATION WILL HEAR OF THIS, I ASSURE YOU! IMLACH OUT!
BUDDA-BUDDA
CAPTAIN--I BELIEVE I HAVE LOCATED THE SOURCE OF THE VIBRATIONS.

THAT WAS QUICK, MISTER DATA.
I AM AN EXCELLENT SWIMMER, SIR.
A WALL, DATA?
MORE SPECIFICALLY, SIR, WHAT IS BEHIND IT.
WHAT HAVE YOU FOUND?
IT APPEARS TO BE A WALL, SIR.
BUDDA-BUDDA
I HOPE TO HAVE ADDITIONAL INFORMATION IN A MOMENT.
WHAT ARE YOU DOING, DATA?
I AM OPENING A DIALOGUE WITH WHATEVER IS BEHIND THE WALL, SIR.
ZZZT!
DATA? ARE YOU ALL RIGHT?
QUITE ALL RIGHT, CAPTAIN. AND I HAVE GOOD NEWS.
I HAVE FOUND COUNSELOR TROI.

"ACTUALLY, THERE IS *ANOTHER* PROBLEM, WORF. WE MUST NOT FORGET THE *HOSTILES.*"

YOU MEAN THEY CAN STILL STOP US. BY LATCHING ONTO OUR SHUTTLE WHEN WE TRY TO TAKE OFF.

OF COURSE. IF YOUR CRAFT DOES NOT LEAVE THE STRUCTURE QUICKLY ENOUGH, THEIR TRACTOR BEAMS WILL DRAG IT BACK. AND THEN WE WILL HAVE TO FIGHT FOR IT ALL OVER AGAIN.

WHAT IS MORE, THERE ARE CORRIDORS UPON CORRIDORS IN THE STRUCTURE, AND WE CANNOT GUARD THEM ALL.

REMEMBER--
I AM A BETAZOID.
I CAN SENSE
SUCH THINGS.
THEN WHY ARE WE STANDING HERE? WHY ARE WE NOT LAUNCHING A PREEMPTIVE STRIKE?

THAT IS NOT OUR WAY, WORF. WE HAVE FOUGHT THE HOSTILES MANY TIMES OVER THE YEARS--
"--AND WE HAVE FOUND THAT THE BEST STRATEGY IS TO FIGHT THEM ON OUR HOME GROUND--WHERE WE KNOW THE INS AND OUTS OF THE SHIPS' DESIGNS."

DARIOS! DARIOS! THE TIME HAS COME--THE HOSTILES ARE APPROACHING THROUGH THE ORMATU HULK!

RIGHT ON SCHEDULE.

THEN IT WAS THEY WHO CREATED THE VIBRATION I HEARD?
YES--BY BATTERING THE WALL WITH THEIR TAILS. I KNEW THE SOUND WOULD REACH YOUR EARS--

THOUGH I WAS NOT SURE IF YOU WOULD KNOW WHAT TO MAKE OF IT.

BUT WHY WOULD THE LANATOSIANS IMPRISON YOU HERE?
BECAUSE THEY DIDN'T WANT THEIR SECRET TO GET BACK TO THE CAPTAIN.

AND WE STILL DON'T! DID YOU THINK WE WOULDN'T FOLLOW YOU, ANDROID?

NOW HAND OVER THAT PHASER--OR WE'LL START BLASTING YOUR NEW FRIENDS!

I HAVE NO CHOICE, COUNSELOR. I CANNOT ALLOW THESE CREATURES TO BE DESTROYED.
I UNDERSTAND, DATA.

AFTER WE GET HIS WEAPON, WE'LL CLOSE UP THE HOLE AGAIN. OUR SECRET WILL STILL BE SAFE...

I BELIEVE YOU WANTED THIS.

I APOLOGIZE-- BUT I CANNOT COMPLY WITH YOUR WISHES.

NOT WHEN IT WOULD MEAN THE FURTHER INCARCERATION OF THESE GENTLE CREATURES.

NOR CAN I ALLOW YOU TO RETAIN YOUR WEAPONS UNDER THE CIRCUMSTANCES.

I HOPE YOU WILL UNDERSTAND.

GOOD WORK, DATA.
THANK YOU, COUNSELOR.
YOU MAY LEAVE IF YOU LIKE--WHICH IS MORE OF A CHOICE THAN YOU GAVE US.
IN FACT, IT MIGHT BE BETTER IF YOU DID LEAVE--TO TELL YOUR SUPERIORS THAT CAPTAIN PICARD IS ON TO THEIR DECEPTION.
WE MUST LEAVE NOW--BUT WE WILL BE BACK. I PROMISE.
WE WILL SEE TO IT THAT YOU DO NOT PERISH HERE!
TROI TO ENTERPRISE. TWO TO BEAM UP.
ENERGIZE!
16

I'M FRIGHTENED, WES.

FRIGHTENED? YOU? YOU'RE A STARFLEET OFFICER. YOU'RE TRAINED FOR THIS SORT OF THING-- AREN'T YOU?

TRAINING IS ONE THING. REALITY IS ANOTHER.

I MEAN, WE COULD DIE HERE. AND NO ONE WOULD EVER KNOW.
DOESN'T THAT SCARE YOU?

TRUTHFULLY?

IT SCARES ME A WHOLE LOT.

I WISH THERE WERE SOME WAY WE COULD COMMUNICATE WITH THESE HOSTILES--MAYBE REACH A COMPROMISE WITH THEM.
BUT DARIOS SAYS THEY'VE TRIED-- AND FAILED.

WOULD YOU DO ME A FAVOR, WES?
SURE-- ANYTHING.

WOULD YOU HOLD ME--JUST FOR A SECOND?

THANK YOU. I FEEL A LITTLE BETTER NOW.
SO DO I.

THEY'RE HERE! THEY'RE ATTACKING THROUGH THE CALUBITE VESSEL!

WHAT?!
YOU HEARD ME, FIRST GOVERNOR. THIS DISCOVERY OF ANOTHER SENTIENT RACE ON LANATOS FORCES A CHANGE IN OUR PLANS.
THE SKRIITI, AS THEY CALL THEMSELVES, MUST OBVIOUSLY BE GIVEN PRIORITY OVER INANIMATE OBJECTS IN OUR EVACUATION EFFORTS. WE ARE THEREFORE DISCONTINUING WORK ON THE MONUMENTS--AND PREPARING LIVING SPACES FOR THE SKRIITI INSTEAD.

THIS IS AN OUTRAGE, CAPTAIN! HOW MANY TIMES MUST I STRESS THE IMPORTANCE OF THOSE MONUMENTS TO OUR CULTURE?
"WHILE THE SKRIITI ARE A PRIMITIVE AND LOATHSOME RACE--ONE THAT WILL NEVER REACH THE LEVEL OF OUR CIVILIZATION!"
WHAT'S MORE, THE BEASTS HAVE PROVEN DANGEROUS--THEY HAVE KILLED. WOULD YOU HAVE US BRING OUR NATURAL ENEMIES ALONG TO OUR NEW HOME?
THE SKRIITI ARE NOT DANGEROUS. WHEN THEY HAVE KILLED, IT HAS BEEN IN SELF-DEFENSE.
OR DO YOU DENY THAT YOU HAVE HUNTED THEM FOR SPORT?
THAT IS BESIDE THE POINT, COMMANDER TROI. IN FACT, ALL OF THIS IS BESIDE THE POINT.
20

MINE IS THE RACE THAT JOINED YOUR FEDERATION. THEREFORE, MINE IS THE RACE TO WHOM YOU OWE *ALLEGIANCE*.

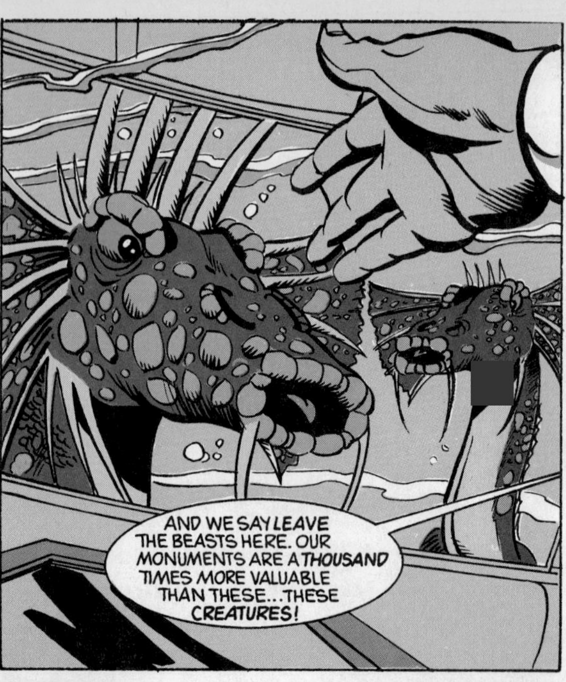
AND WE SAY *LEAVE* THE BEASTS HERE. OUR MONUMENTS ARE A *THOUSAND* TIMES MORE VALUABLE THAN THESE... THESE *CREATURES!*

IT IS TRUE THAT YOU HAVE AN AGREEMENT WITH THE FEDERATION-- BUT IT WAS NEVER MEANT TO *EXCLUDE* OTHER SENTIENT RACES ON YOUR PLANET.

IT WOULD BE THE GRAVEST OF INJUSTICES TO SACRIFICE *INTELLIGENT* BEINGS--

--FOR THE SAKE OF A PILE OF *STONES*. AND FRANKLY, GIVEN YOUR APPALLING DISREGARD FOR THE VALUE OF LIFE--

--YOU SHOULD CONSIDER YOURSELVES FORTUNATE THAT I AM NOT LEAVING *YOU* BEHIND!

THIS WAY! THAT'S WHERE WE SPOTTED THEM!
I HAVE A BAD FEELING ABOUT THIS.
BAD IN WHAT WAY?
I SENSE THAT WE ARE WALKING INTO A *TRAP*.
RRRGH!

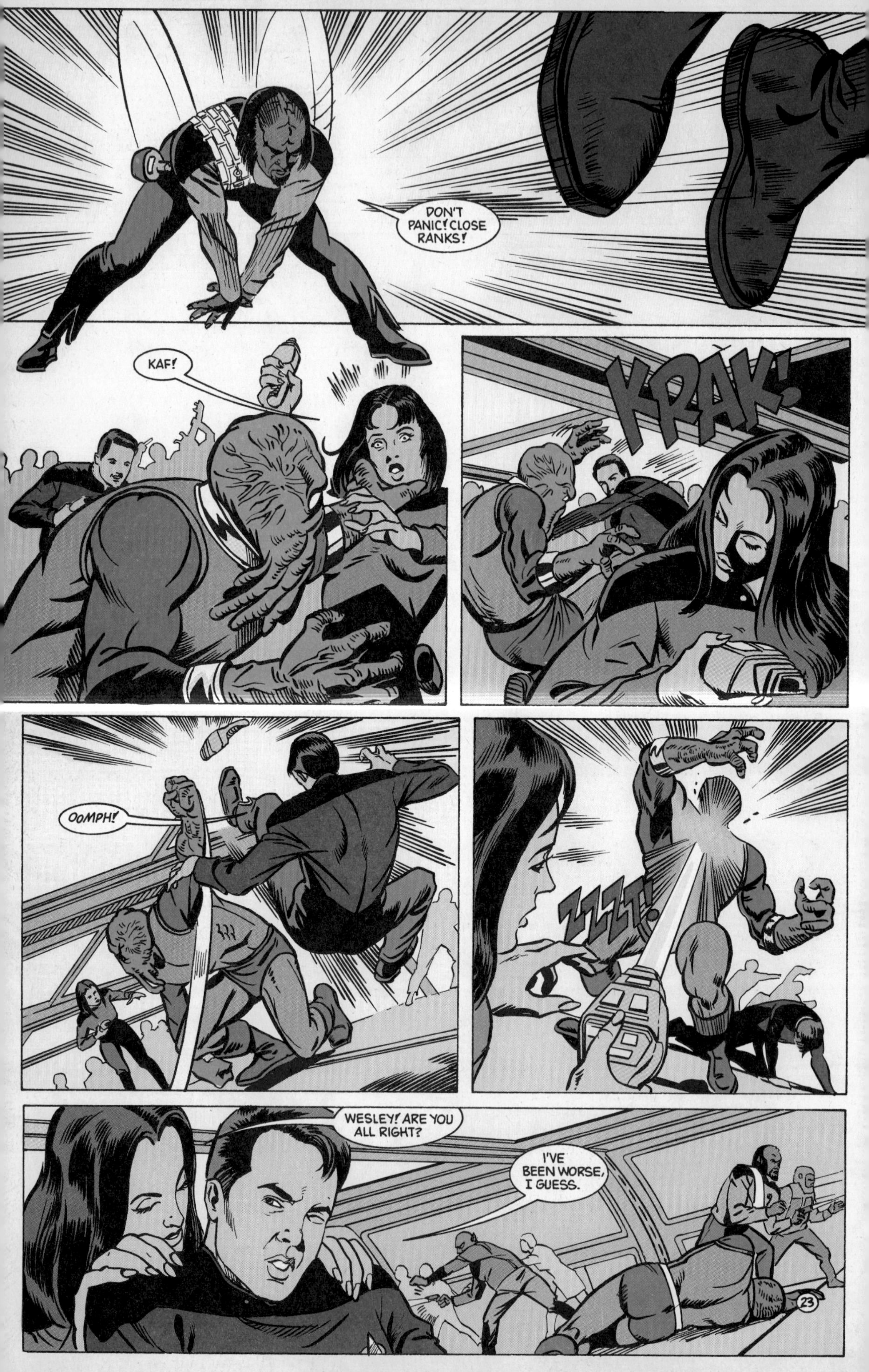

DON'T PANIC! CLOSE RANKS!

KAF!

KRAK!

ARRH!
AIEEE!
GRRR!
HOW STRANGE! A KLINGON-- FIGHTING WITH THE ENEMY!
I WAS JUST THINKING THE SAME THING OF YOU!
TO BE CONTINUED

HOMECOMING
MICHAEL JAN FRIEDMAN WRITER
PETER KRAUSE PENCILLER
PABLO MARCOS INKER
BOB PINAHA LETTERER
JULIANNA FERRITER COLORIST
ROBERT GREENBERGER EDITOR
HOLD THEM! THEY MUST NOT GET PAST US!
BASED ON STAR TREK: THE NEXT GENERATION CREATED BY GENE RODDENBERRY!

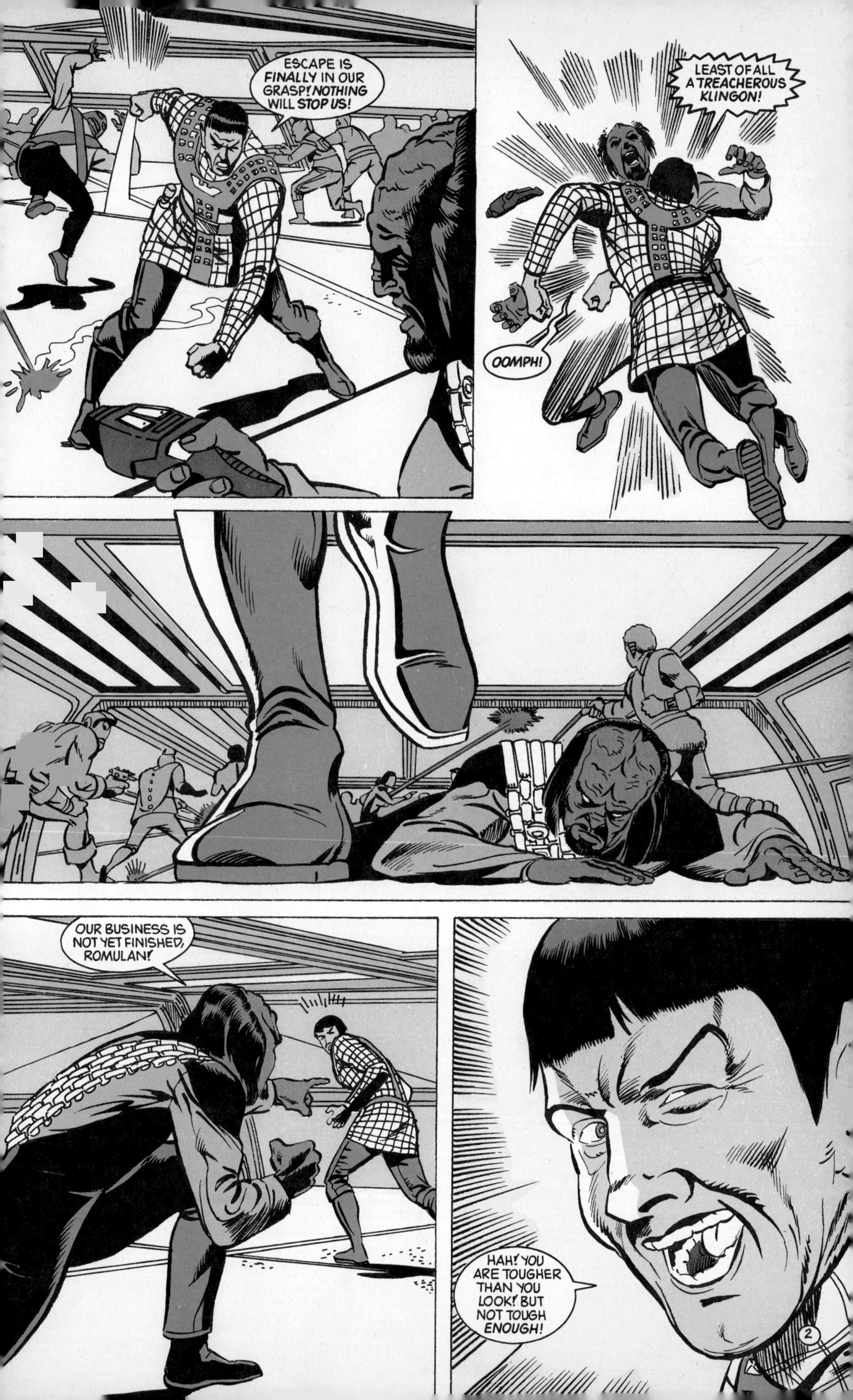

ESCAPE IS FINALLY IN OUR GRASP! NOTHING WILL STOP US!
LEAST OF ALL A TREACHEROUS KLINGON!
OOMPH!

THAT IS
A MATTER OF
OPINION!

AND
HERE IS
EVIDENCE
TO THE
CONTRARY!
UNNH!

ELOQUENT, IS
IT NOT?
UNNGH!

NO MATTER.
YOU WILL NOT
WITHSTAND
THIS!

ST-TNG!

ZZZT!

THEY'RE RETREATING--
"--WE'VE WON!"
BUT NOT FOR LONG. THEY WILL BE BACK!
AND NEXT TIME, THEY MAY GET WHAT THEY'RE AFTER. WE MUST BEGIN USING THE SHUTTLE--
"--TO TRANSPORT OUR PEOPLE TO THE ALIEN SHIP."
MISTER CRUSHER-- ENSIGN NIGATA--YOU ARE WITH ME.
AYE, SIR.

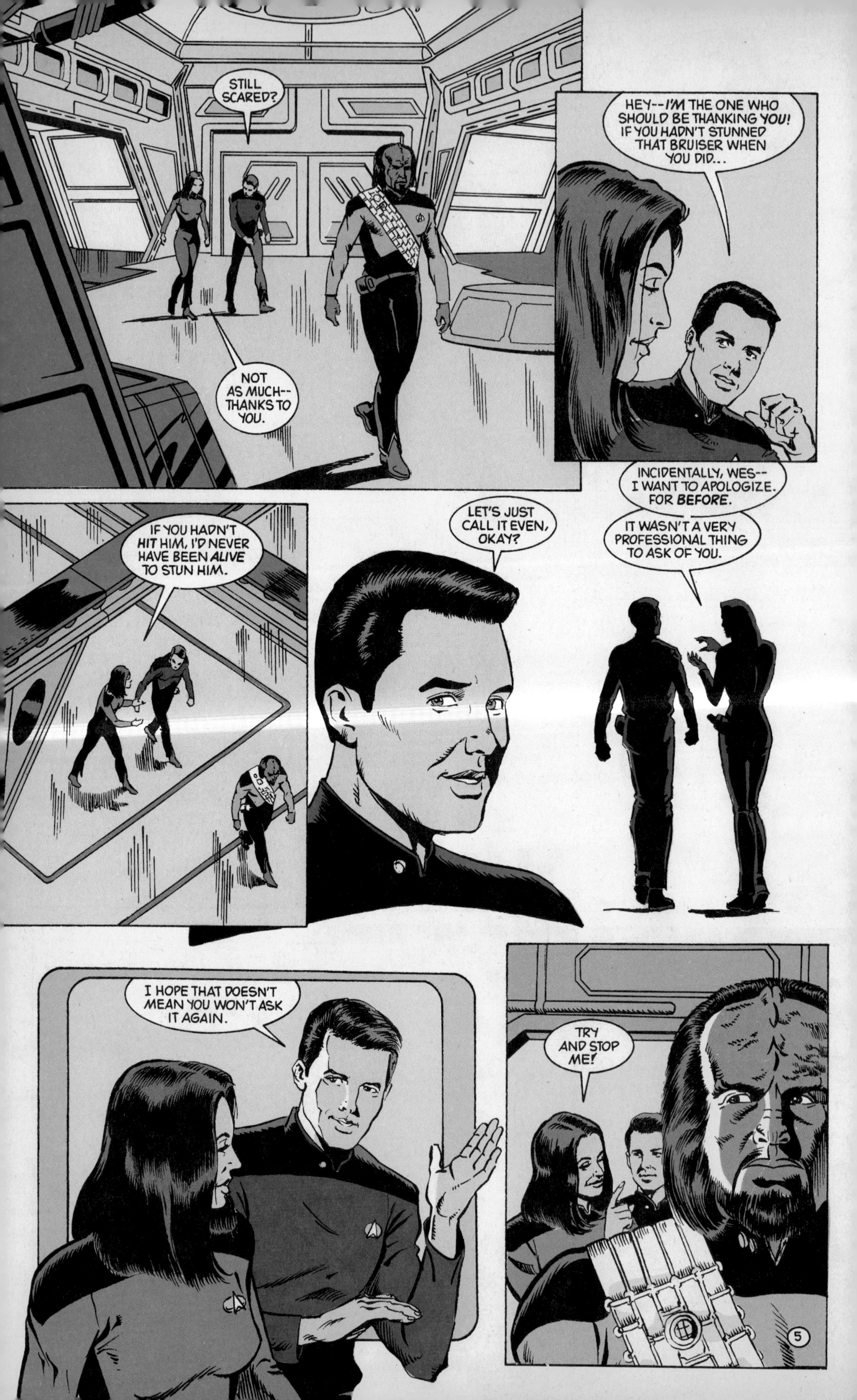

STILL SCARED?

NOT AS MUCH-- THANKS TO YOU.

HEY--*I'M* THE ONE WHO SHOULD BE THANKING *YOU!* IF YOU HADN'T STUNNED THAT BRUISER WHEN YOU DID...

IF YOU HADN'T *HIT* HIM, I'D NEVER HAVE BEEN *ALIVE* TO STUN HIM.

LET'S JUST CALL IT EVEN, OKAY?

INCIDENTALLY, WES-- I WANT TO APOLOGIZE. FOR *BEFORE*.

IT WASN'T A VERY PROFESSIONAL THING TO ASK OF YOU.

"THAT WAS OUR *HOME*."
IT IS DIFFICULT TO WITNESS THE DEATH OF ONE'S *PLANET*--
--A BIT LIKE WATCHING THE DEATH OF A LOVED ONE.
DON'T COMPARE A PLANET WITH A PERSON, FIRST GOVERNOR.
PLANETS ARE BALLS OF MUD-- *THINGS*. THEY CAN BE REPLACED.
WHEN A PERSON IS GONE, HE'S GONE *FOREVER*.
6

WE HAVE DIFFERENT WAYS OF LOOKING AT SUCH MATTERS, DOCTOR. ON MY WORLD--WHAT USED TO BE MY WORLD--WE RISKED OUR LIVES FOR THINGS.
OUR MONUMENTS, FOR INSTANCE. EVEN NOW, I WOULD GLADLY FORFEIT MY LIFE TO HAVE THEM BACK AGAIN.
NOR HAVE I CHANGED MY MIND ABOUT LODGING A PROTEST WITH THE FEDERATION. TO LEAVE BEHIND SUCH GREAT WORKS OF ART... IN ORDER TO TAKE ALONG A HERD OF BEASTS...
--IS WELL WITHIN MY RANGE OF DISCRETION, FIRST GOVERNOR.
STILL, PROTEST IF YOU LIKE. IT IS CERTAINLY YOUR RIGHT.
BUT IF I WERE YOU, I WOULD BE CONCENTRATING ON MY NEW HOME--BETA DIOMEDE FOUR. I WOULD BE LOOKING TO THE FUTURE, NOT THE PAST.
AND I WOULD BE LOOKING TO THE SKRIITI FOR WHAT-EVER HELP THEY COULD GIVE ME.
7

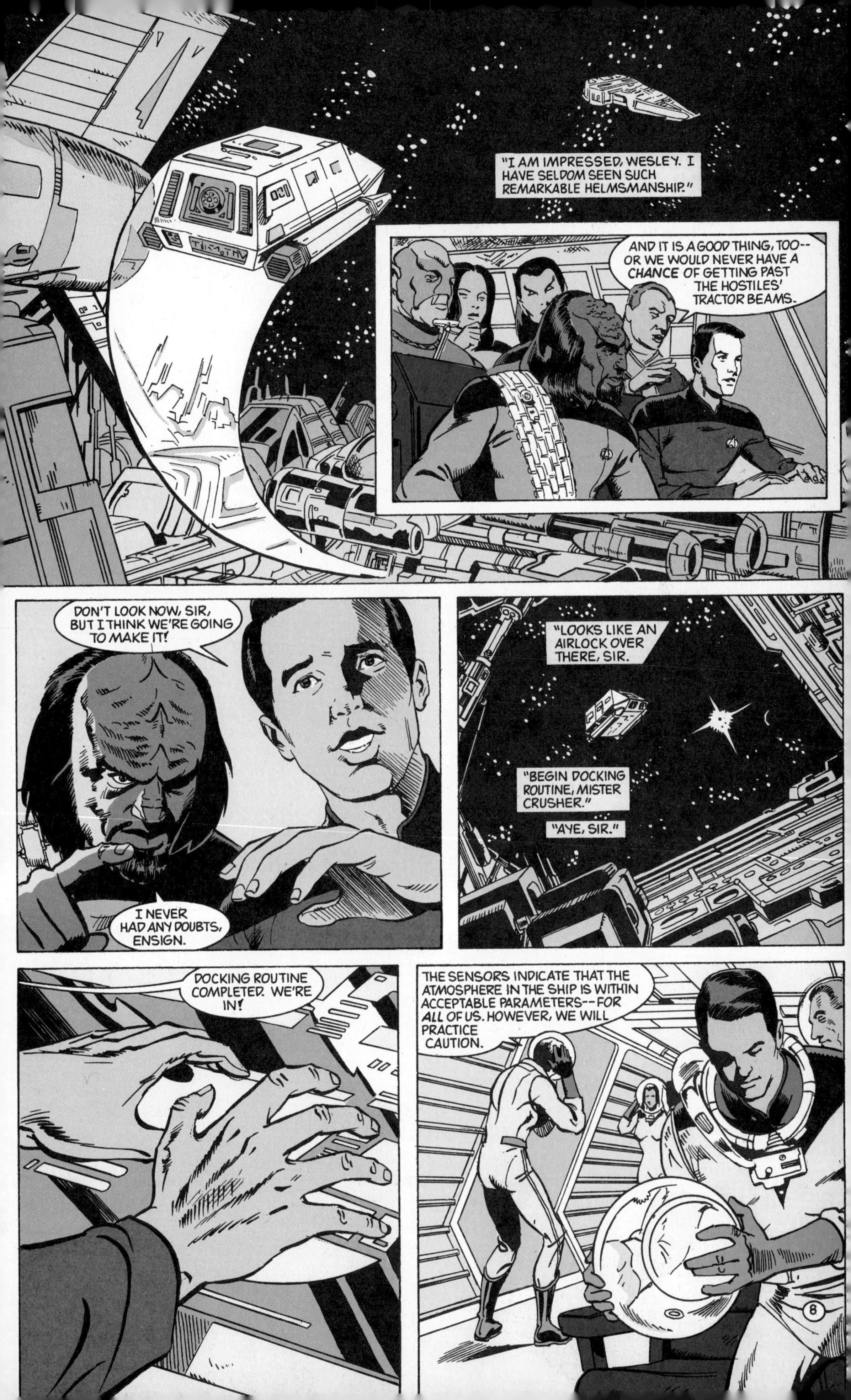

"I AM IMPRESSED, WESLEY. I HAVE SELDOM SEEN SUCH REMARKABLE HELMSMANSHIP."

AND IT IS A GOOD THING, TOO--OR WE WOULD NEVER HAVE A *CHANCE* OF GETTING PAST THE HOSTILES' TRACTOR BEAMS.

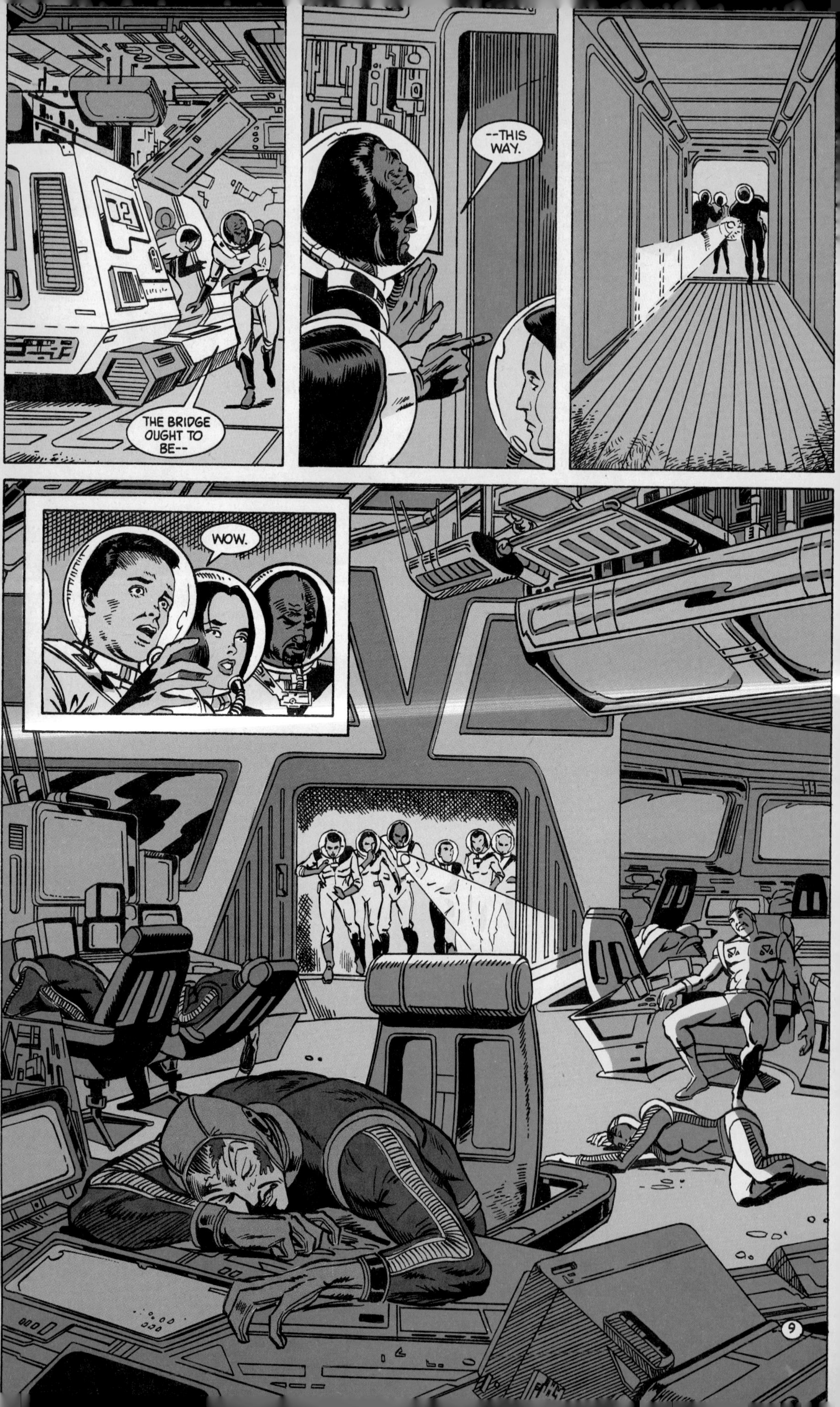

WOW.

THE SENSORS WERE RIGHT. THIS ATMOSPHERE IS EMINENTLY BREATHABLE.
NOT THAT IT DID *THEM* ANY GOOD.
THE VORTEX MUST HAVE HANDLED *THIS* SHIP A LOT MORE ROUGHLY THAN IT DID OURS.
COMMUNICATIONS ARE BEYOND REPAIR. WE WILL HAVE TO DO WITHOUT THEM.
THERE'S SOME DAMAGE HERE TOO--BUT THE WARP DRIVE SEEMS INTACT. AND IT'S GOT PLENTY OF POWER IN RESERVE.
GOOD. IN THE MEANTIME, WE WILL SEE IF THOSE WHO DESIGNED THIS SHIP HAD THE *FORESIGHT* TO INCLUDE A *TRANSPORTER* FACILITY.
OF COURSE, I HAVEN'T GOT THE SLIGHTEST IDEA OF HOW TO *OPERATE* IT--BUT I SUPPOSE I CAN LEARN.

DOCTOR SELAR!
WHAT IS IT, NURSE?
HE'S AWAKE! HE'S COME OUT OF IT!
MUST...
YOU MUST DO NOTHING--EXCEPT REST.
SHUTTLE... CREW...?
ALL FINE--EXCEPT YOU. WE ARE A LONG WAY FROM THE ENTERPRISE--BUT WE ARE TRYING TO FIND OUR WAY BACK.
BACK...YES... BACK...

SADNESS INSIDE...
BUT WHY? YOU ARE SAFE. YOU ARE HEADED FOR A NEW HOME.

NOT IN ME, LITTLE ONE... IN YOU...

YOU ARE VERY PERCEPTIVE, MY FRIEND. YES--I AM SAD INSIDE.

I HAVE LOST SOME OF MY FRIENDS. I WILL NEVER SEE THEM AGAIN.

AND THIS MAKES YOU SAD...I UNDERSTAND...

...IT IS A HARD THING... WHEN THE HERD IS DIMINISHED...

...BUT FOR THE SAKE OF THOSE WHO ARE LEFT... WE MUST GO ON...

"FINALLY, THE EXODUS IS COMPLETE. IT IS FORTUNATE THAT THIS SHIP HAD A TRANSPORTER FACILITY-- THAT IT WAS NOT TOO DIFFERENT FROM THAT OF THE *ENTERPRISE*-- AND THAT IT *WORKED.*"
HOWEVER, I STILL HAVE A DECISION TO MAKE. CAN I RETURN HOME WITHOUT BRINGING ALONG MY KLINGON BROTHERS--DESPITE THE FACT THAT THEY WOULD WRING MY NECK, GIVEN HALF A CHANCE?
THERE IS A BIGGER QUESTION HERE, WORF. REMEMBER--THERE ARE OTHERS BESIDES KLINGONS AMONG THE HOSTILES.
CAN YOU LEAVE THEM HERE, PERHAPS NEVER TO SEE THEIR HOMES AGAIN? DO YOU WANT THAT ON YOUR CONSCIENCE?
THEY ARE YOUR *ENEMIES!* THEY HAVE SPILLED THE BLOOD OF YOUR PEOPLE!
THE WAR IS *OVER.* WHY NOT BE MERCIFUL IN VICTORY?
MISTER CRUSHER-- HOLD YOUR POSITION.

ATTENTION, YOU WHO SO RECENTLY SOUGHT TO DESTROY US!

WE HAVE REACHED THE ALIEN SHIP DESPITE YOU...
SHUT IT OFF! I DO NOT WISH TO HEAR ANY MORE!
NO--WAIT! HE CANNOT BE CALLING JUST TO GLOAT!
WHY NOT? HE IS A KLINGON, ISN'T HE?

...BUT WE ARE WILLING TO SHARE IN OUR GOOD FORTUNE. IF YOU DROP YOUR SHIELDS, WE WILL BEAM YOU TO OUR CARGO HOLD--AND BRING YOU WITH US AS WE TRY TO RETURN THE WAY WE CAME.
NCC-170

WHAT KIND OF FOOLS DOES HE TAKE US FOR? IF WE DROP OUR SHIELDS, HE WILL ANNIHILATE US!
YOU ARE THE FOOL! IS IT NOT WORTH THE RISK-- FOR A CHANCE TO GO HOME AGAIN?

A KLINGON WOULD NOT RESORT TO SUCH A COWARDLY PLOY-- NOT EVEN A KLINGON WHO FIGHTS ON THE SIDE OF THE FEDERATION!
I SAY WE TRUST HIM!

WE ACCEPT YOUR OFFER! LOWER THE SHIELDS!
VERY WELL. PREPARE...

"...FOR TRANSPORT."
THAT'S THE LAST OF 'EM, SIR.
WELL DONE, MISTER O'BRIEN.
I GUESS I'LL START ON THE SKRIITI NOW, EH?
BY ALL MEANS, CHIEF.
I WILL MISS THE SKRIITI. THEY WERE GOOD COMPANIONS.
YES--YOU SPENT QUITE A BIT OF TIME WITH THEM, DIDN'T YOU?
"IT WAS TIME WELL-SPENT. SOMETIMES EVEN A SHIP'S COUNSELOR NEEDS SOMEONE TO TALK TO...
"...CAPTAIN--DO YOU THINK THE LANATOSIANS WILL TAKE YOUR ADVICE--ABOUT WORKING TOGETHER WITH THE SKRIITI TO BUILD THEIR NEW WORLD?"

"PERHAPS NOT RIGHT AWAY. PERHAPS NOT EVEN IN THIS GENERATION.
"BUT IN TIME, I THINK IT *WILL* HAPPEN."
AS ALWAYS, CAPTAIN, YOU INSPIRE CONFIDENCE.
ABOUT THAT OTHER MATTER WE WERE DISCUSSING, CAPTAIN...
WHAT OTHER MATTER IS THAT, COUNSELOR?
THE MATTER OF REPLACING COMMANDER RIKER AND LIEUTENANT WORF.
AH. *THAT* MATTER.
16

LAST TIME WE SPOKE, YOU SAID THAT YOU WOULD PROMOTE COMMANDER DATA AND MISTER BURKE AS SOON AS WE WERE FINISHED WITH OUR ASSIGNMENT ON LANATOS.
WE LEFT LANATOS TWO DAYS AGO. AND NEITHER DATA NOR BURKE HAVE BEEN NOTIFIED.
BRIDGE.
IF I DID NOT KNOW BETTER, I WOULD SAY YOU ARE STILL DENYING THE DEATHS OF THOSE ON THE EINSTEIN.
BUT OF COURSE, I DO KNOW BETTER--DON'T I, CAPTAIN?
I KNOW--I HAVE BEEN DERELICT IN THIS REGARD. AND I INTEND TO MAKE UP FOR IT--
--JUST AS SOON AS WE FINISH BEAMING DOWN THE LANATOSIANS.

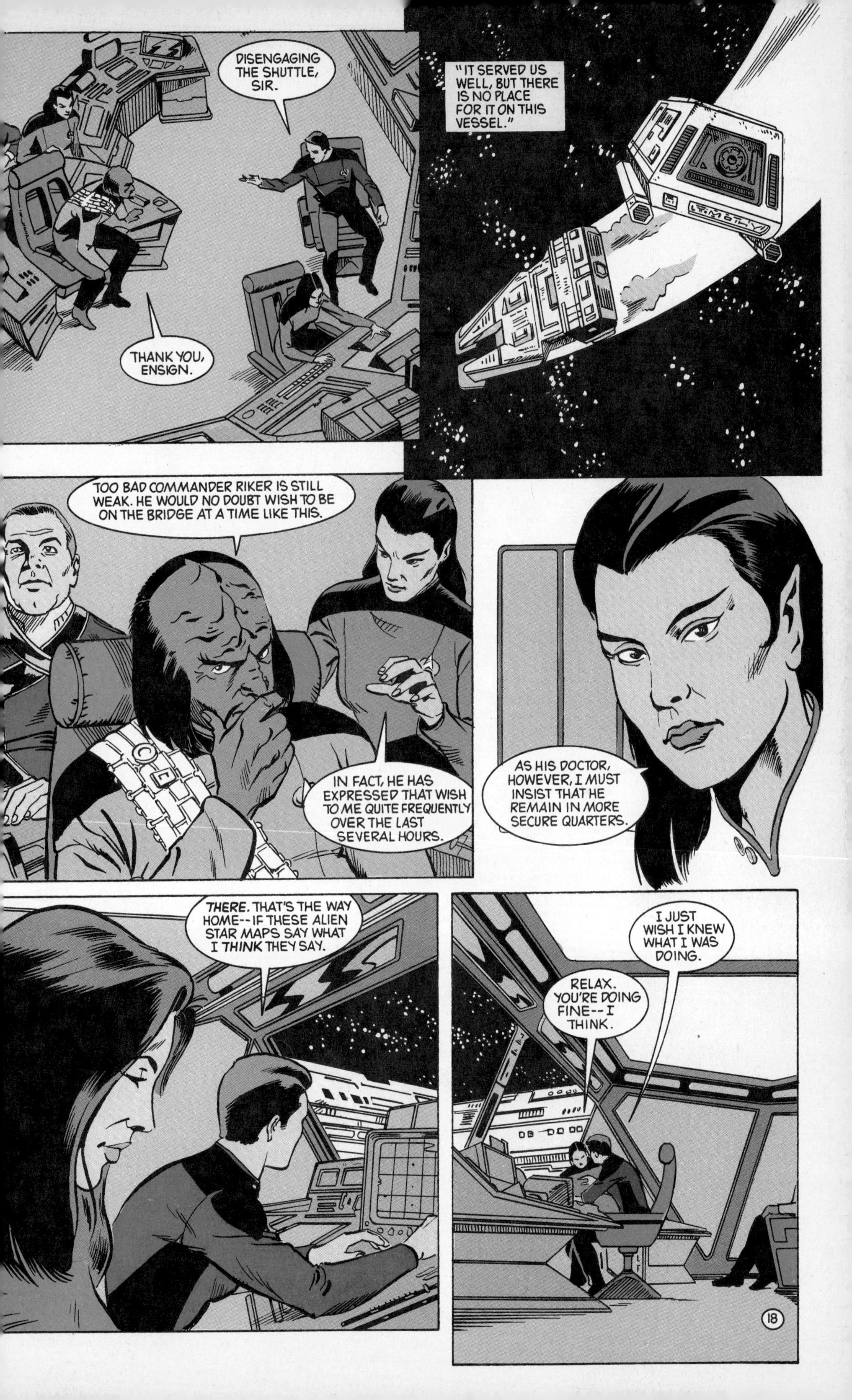

DISENGAGING THE SHUTTLE, SIR.
THANK YOU, ENSIGN.
"IT SERVED US WELL, BUT THERE IS NO PLACE FOR IT ON THIS VESSEL."

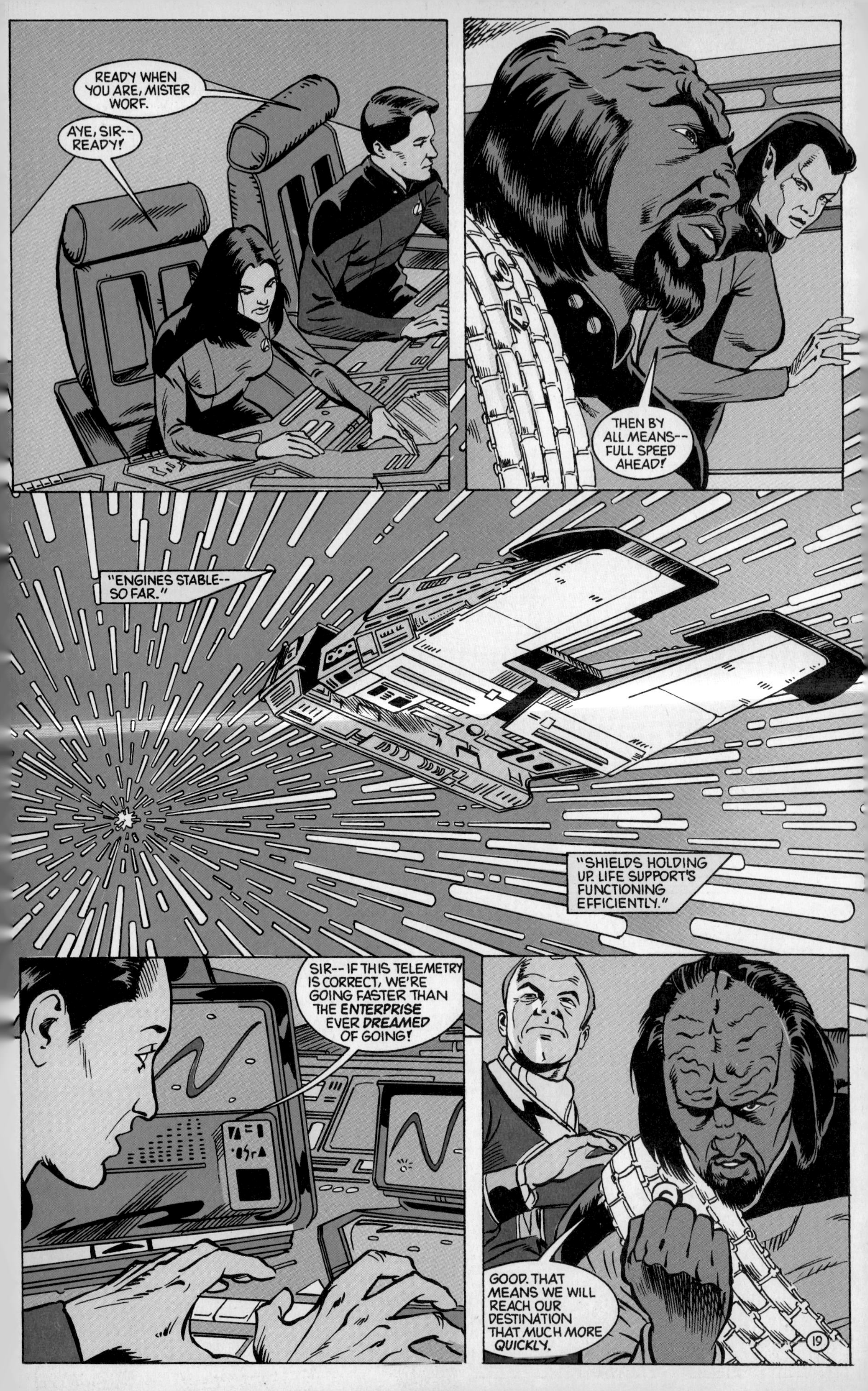
READY WHEN YOU ARE, MISTER WORF.
AYE, SIR-- READY!
THEN BY ALL MEANS-- FULL SPEED AHEAD!
"ENGINES STABLE-- SO FAR."
"SHIELDS HOLDING UP. LIFE SUPPORT'S FUNCTIONING EFFICIENTLY."
SIR-- IF THIS TELEMETRY IS CORRECT, WE'RE GOING FASTER THAN THE ENTERPRISE EVER DREAMED OF GOING!
GOOD. THAT MEANS WE WILL REACH OUR DESTINATION THAT MUCH MORE QUICKLY.

ONLY ONE PROBLEM, SIR. I'VE FIGURED OUT HOW TO STOP US--BUT NOT HOW TO SLOW US DOWN.
AND AS FAST AS WE'RE TRAVELING, THERE'S GOING TO BE A LAG BETWEEN THE TIME WE SIGHT A FAMILIAR CONSTELLATION--AND THE TIME WE CAN REACT TO IT.
I UNDERSTAND, ENSIGN. FORTUNATELY, WE HAVE A GREAT DEAL OF LATITUDE IN THAT REGARD. UNDER THE CIRCUMSTANCES, I WILL BE HAPPY TO ARRIVE ANYWHERE IN THE FEDERATION.
"AT THE SPEED WE'RE GOING, I CAN'T GUARANTEE WE'LL WIND UP IN THE FEDERATION AT ALL."
WHAT ARE YOU SAYING, ENSIGN? THAT WE MIGHT FIND OURSELVES AMONG THE ROMULANS? OR THE BORG?
IT'S A POSSIBILITY, SIR.

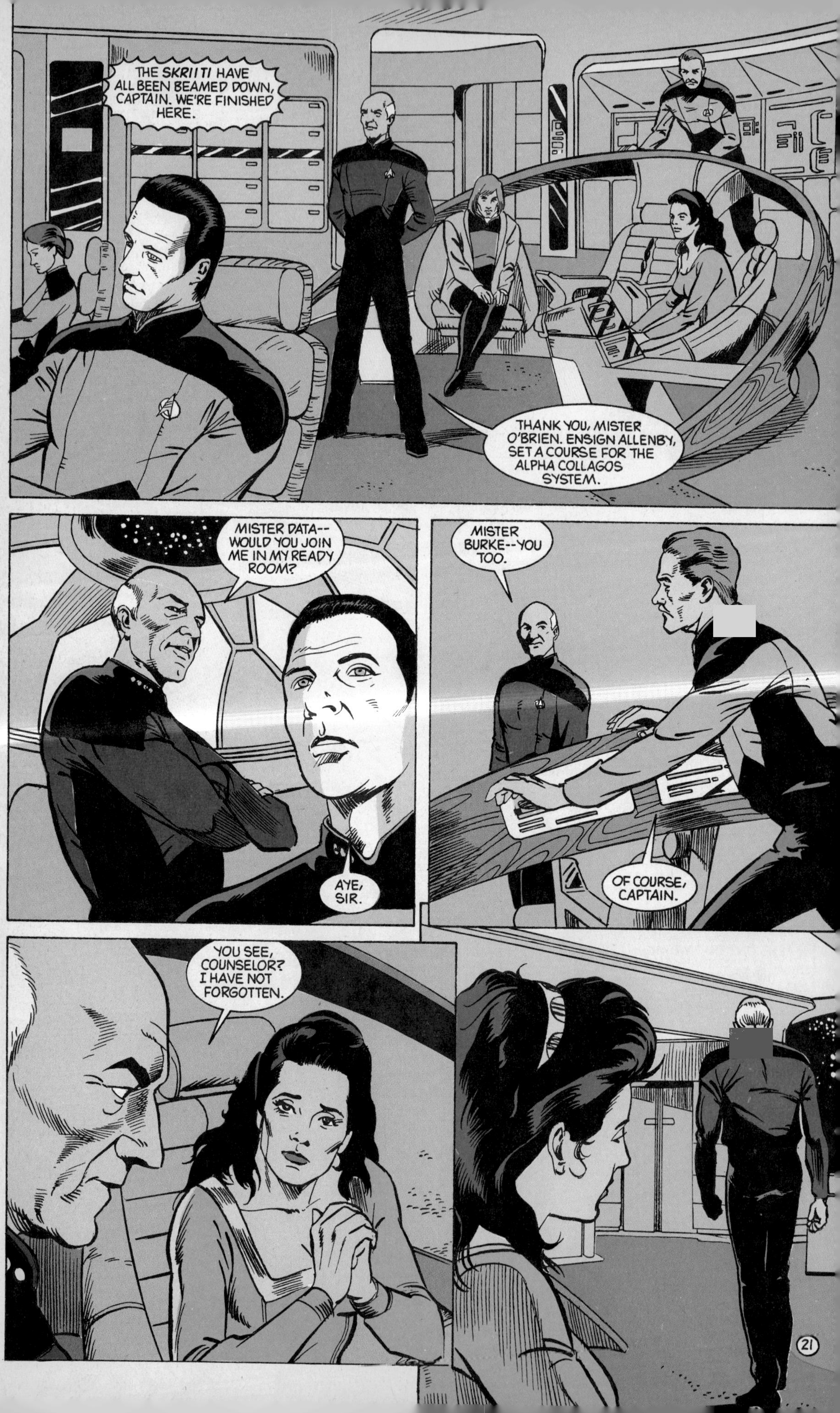

THE *SKRIITI* HAVE ALL BEEN BEAMED DOWN, CAPTAIN. WE'RE FINISHED HERE.

THANK YOU, MISTER O'BRIEN. ENSIGN ALLENBY, SET A COURSE FOR THE ALPHA COLLAGOS SYSTEM.

"UH-OH. SOMETHING'S WRONG.
"WHAT IS IT, MISTER CRUSHER?"
IT'S THE ENGINES. THEY'RE CUTTING OUT. SO MUCH FOR WORRYING ABOUT WHERE WE'RE GOING TO STOP--I THINK THE SHIP HAS MADE THAT DECISION FOR US!
READINGS COMING IN NOW FROM ASTROGATION...
...WELL, HOW ABOUT THAT!
"WHERE ARE WE, ENSIGN?"
"ALMOST HOME, SIR."
RIGHT IN THE CENTER OF THE KLINGON EMPIRE--LESS THAN A PARSEC FROM THE KLINGON HOMEWORLD!
THE KLINGON... HOMEWORLD?! ALL AVAILABLE POWER TO THE SHIELDS!
22

I DON'T UNDERSTAND, DOCTOR. AREN'T THE KLINGONS OUR ALLIES NOW?
YES. BUT HOW WILL THEY KNOW IT IS US IN HERE?
"ALL THEY WILL SEE IS AN INVADER--A STRANGE SHIP THAT POSES A THREAT TO THEIR HOME-WORLD. AND WITH OUR COMMUNICATIONS EQUIPMENT DOWN, WE WILL NOT BE ABLE TO TELL THEM OTHERWISE."

I SEE. THEN WE ARE IN DANGER.

DAMN! IF YOU THINK THAT'S TROUBLE, YOU OUGHT TO TAKE A LOOK AT THIS!

THE ENGINES DIDN'T JUST SHUT DOWN--THEY OVERLOADED! AND THE OVERLOAD IS BUILDING-- I CAN'T STOP IT!

IF WE DON'T GET OFF THIS SHIP SOON, THE KLINGONS WON'T HAVE TO DESTROY US! WE'LL JUST BLOW UP!

I WILL NOT TELL YOU THIS IS A HAPPY MOMENT FOR ME, GENTLEMEN. IT MEANS ACCEPTING THE LOSS OF TWO OF MY FINEST OFFICERS.

HOWEVER, IF I MUST TURN THEIR POSITIONS OVER TO *SOMEONE*, THERE ARE NO TWO CREWMEN MORE DESERVING--
CAPTAIN...?

WHAT IS IT, ENSIGN ALLENBY?
INCOMING SUBSPACE MESSAGE, SIR. I THINK YOU *MAY* WANT TO SEE IT. IT'S FROM THE *KLINGON* EMPIRE.

VERY WELL, ENSIGN. I WILL TAKE IT HERE. PATCH IT THROUGH TO ME.
AYE, SIR.

THIS IS COMMANDER KROGH OF THE KLINGON VESSEL *ARS'LEK*, CALLING WHICHEVER FEDERATION SHIP IS NEAREST TO OUR BORDER.

WE HAVE DISCOVERED AN UNIDENTIFIED VESSEL IN OUR TERRITORY. AS HONORABLE ALLIES, WE FEEL IT IS OUR DUTY TO INFORM YOU OF THIS FACT--ON THE OFF CHANCE THAT IT IS A FEDERATION SHIP THAT HAS GONE ASTRAY.

WE ARE RELAYING COORDINATES. IF WE DO NOT HEAR FROM *YOU* SHORTLY, WE WILL HAVE NO CHOICE BUT TO *ELIMINATE* THE INVADER! KROGH OUT.
24

"THEY'RE STILL NOT ATTACKING. THEY SEEM TO BE WAITING FOR SOMETHING."
"THERE'S ANOTHER SHIP ARRIVING. SIR--"
--IT LOOKS LIKE A FEDERATION VESSEL--GALAXY CLASS!
COULD IT BE...?
WHAT AM I SAYING? WE'RE GOING TO EXPLODE--AND TAKE EVERY VESSEL IN THE VICINITY WITH US!
IF ONLY THERE WERE A WAY TO WARN THEM--ALL OF THEM!
25

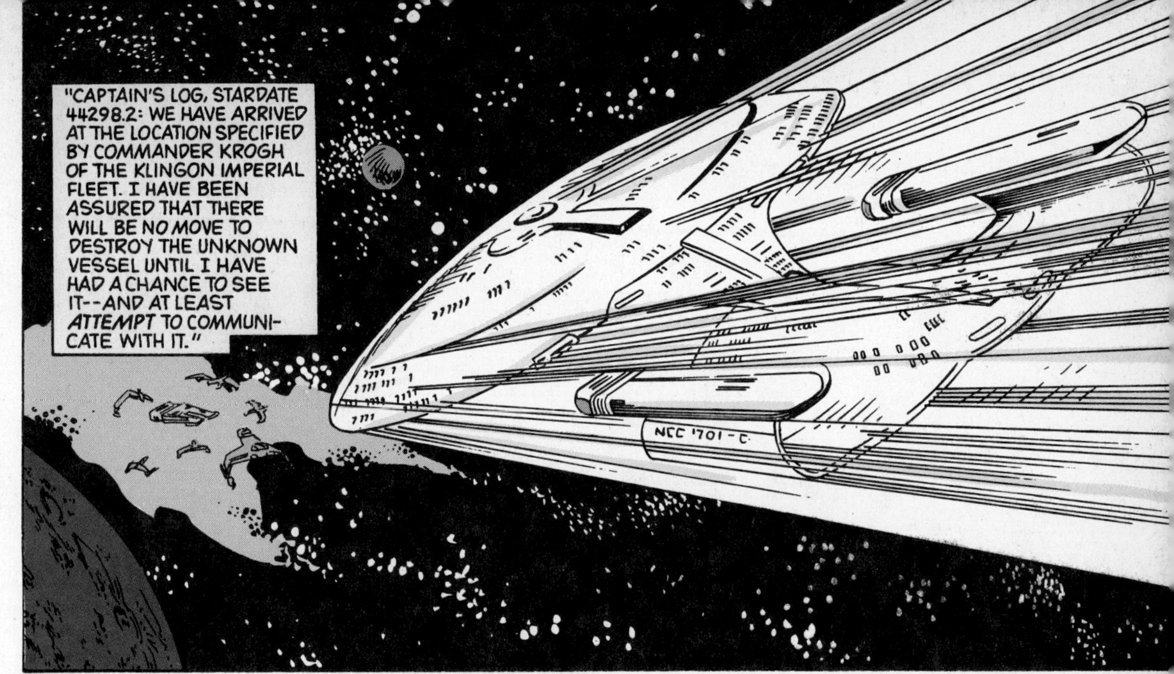
"CAPTAIN'S LOG, STARDATE 44298.2: WE HAVE ARRIVED AT THE LOCATION SPECIFIED BY COMMANDER KROGH OF THE KLINGON IMPERIAL FLEET. I HAVE BEEN ASSURED THAT THERE WILL BE NO MOVE TO DESTROY THE UNKNOWN VESSEL UNTIL I HAVE HAD A CHANCE TO SEE IT--AND AT LEAST ATTEMPT TO COMMUNICATE WITH IT."
NCC 1701-C

"THERE THEY ARE NOW, SIR."
"ISOLATE THE UNKNOWN SHIP FOR ME, ENSIGN. MAGNIFICATION LEVEL THREE."

SENSOR SCAN?
NO READINGS, CAPTAIN. SENSORS CANNOT PENETRATE THE VESSEL'S HULL.

COUNSELOR--WHAT IS IT?
SIR--THAT SHIP IS OCCUPIED BY KLINGONS!

NO--WAIT! NOT JUST KLINGONS! ALSO ROMULANS... FERENGI... HUMANS... BENZITES...

...CAPTAIN--
THERE ARE BETAZOIDS ON THE VESSEL!
DEANNA... IT SEEMS STRANGE THAT SO MANY RACES SHOULD OCCUPY THE SAME SHIP.
I CANNOT EXPLAIN IT. BUT I SENSE TWO FEELINGS VERY STRONGLY.
ONE IS RELIEF.
THE OTHER IS FEAR!
"NOT SURPRISING, UNDER THE CIRCUMSTANCES. THEY'RE STARING INTO THE PHASER BANKS OF HALF A DOZEN KLINGON BATTLE CRUISERS."
NO, CAPTAIN. IT'S NOT JUST THE KLINGONS THEY FEAR. THERE'S SOMETHING ELSE...
"...IT'S AS IF THE SHIP ITSELF PRESENTS A DANGER TO THEM."

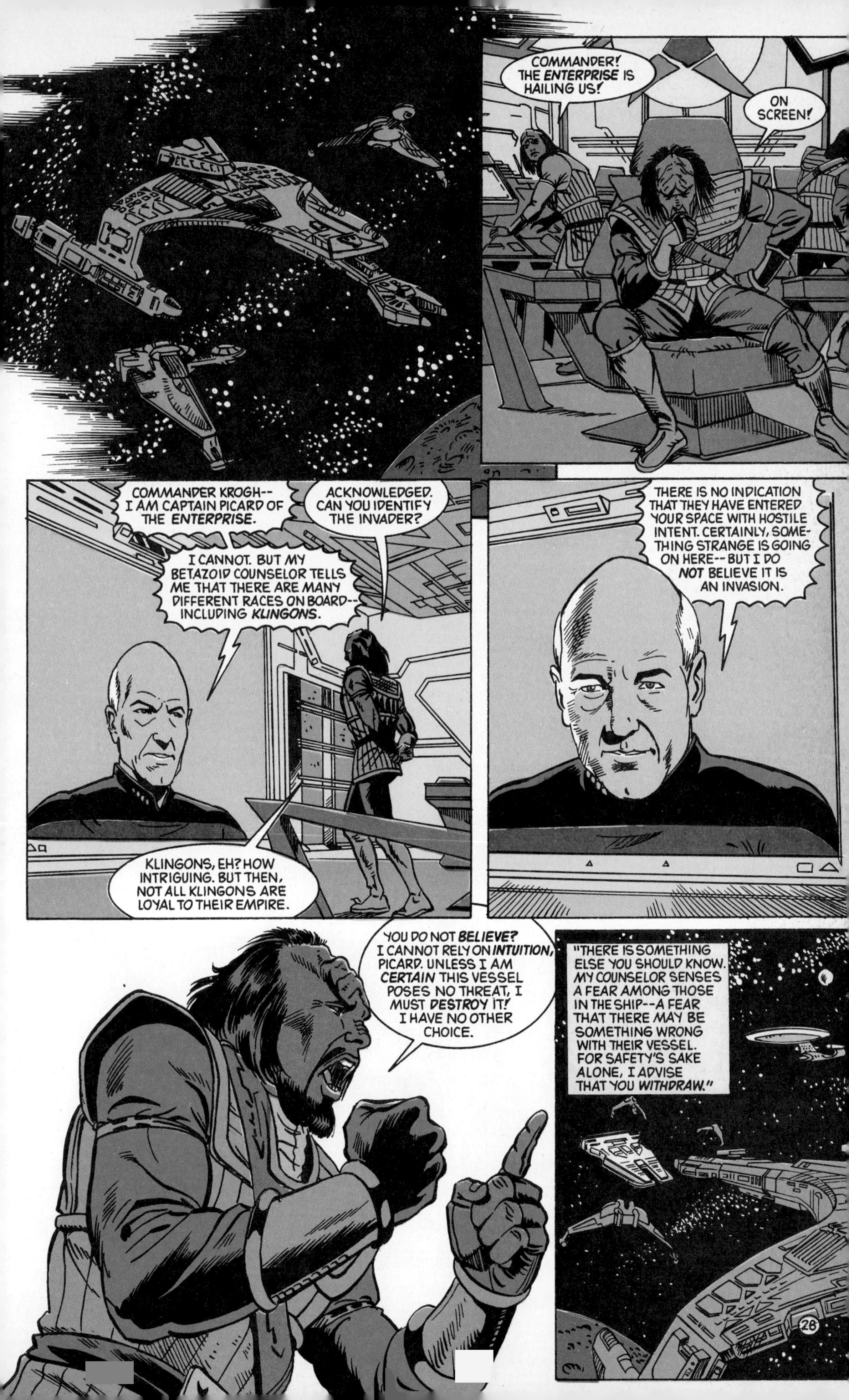
COMMANDER! THE ENTERPRISE IS HAILING US!
ON SCREEN!
COMMANDER KROGH-- I AM CAPTAIN PICARD OF THE ENTERPRISE.
ACKNOWLEDGED. CAN YOU IDENTIFY THE INVADER?
I CANNOT. BUT MY BETAZOID COUNSELOR TELLS ME THAT THERE ARE MANY DIFFERENT RACES ON BOARD-- INCLUDING KLINGONS.
KLINGONS, EH? HOW INTRIGUING. BUT THEN, NOT ALL KLINGONS ARE LOYAL TO THEIR EMPIRE.
THERE IS NO INDICATION THAT THEY HAVE ENTERED YOUR SPACE WITH HOSTILE INTENT. CERTAINLY, SOMETHING STRANGE IS GOING ON HERE-- BUT I DO NOT BELIEVE IT IS AN INVASION.
YOU DO NOT BELIEVE? I CANNOT RELY ON INTUITION, PICARD. UNLESS I AM CERTAIN THIS VESSEL POSES NO THREAT, I MUST DESTROY IT! I HAVE NO OTHER CHOICE.
"THERE IS SOMETHING ELSE YOU SHOULD KNOW. MY COUNSELOR SENSES A FEAR AMONG THOSE IN THE SHIP--A FEAR THAT THERE MAY BE SOMETHING WRONG WITH THEIR VESSEL. FOR SAFETY'S SAKE ALONE, I ADVISE THAT YOU WITHDRAW."
26

THE SECURITY OF THE HOMEWORLD ITSELF IS IN JEOPARDY! IF WE MUST DIE ENSURING THAT SECURITY--SO BE IT!
WITHDRAW--?! NEVER!
A KLINGON COMMANDER DOES NOT RUN WHEN HIS EMPIRE IS IN DANGER.
HE IS ADAMANT, CAPTAIN. UNLESS HE HAS PROOF, HE WILL DESTROY THE SHIP.
THEN I WILL HAVE TO GIVE HIM PROOF.
COMMANDER--WHAT IF I WERE TO BOARD THIS MYSTERIOUS VESSEL? AND SEND YOU A SIGNAL THAT ITS OCCUPANTS MEAN YOU NO HARM? WOULD YOU HOLD YOUR FIRE?
I WOULD--IF YOU COULD DO THAT. WHAT SORT OF SIGNAL DID YOU HAVE IN MIND?
GIVE ME TWENTY MINUTES. THE SIGNAL WILL BE THE DROPPING OF THE SHIP'S SHIELDS.

VERY WELL. TWENTY MINUTES. AND IF I HAVE NOT SEEN THE SIGNAL BY THEN, I WILL DO WHAT I *MUST*. KROGH OUT.
CHIEF O'BRIEN-- I WANT TO TRANSPORT TO THE ALIEN SHIP. FIND ME THE RIGHT HARMONICS.
MISTER DATA--YOU HAVE THE CONN.
SIR? MAY I ACCOMPANY YOU TO THE TRANSPORTER ROOM?
YOU MAY.
TRANSPORTER ROOM ONE. NOW, WHAT IS IT, COMMANDER?
SIR, WITH COMMANDER RIKER GONE, I MUST ASSUME HIS RESPONSIBILITIES IN SOME AREAS.
AND I AM CERTAIN THAT COMMANDER RIKER WOULD NOT HAVE TAKEN YOUR DECISION LIGHTLY. IT IS QUITE A DANGEROUS TASK YOU ARE UNDERTAKING.
YOU BEAMING INTO A SITUATION YOU KNOW NOTHING ABOUT. EVEN ASIDE FROM THE RATHER OMINOUS PRESENCE OF ROMULANS AND FERENGI ABOARD THE VESSEL--

--THERE IS THE MATTER OF THE TRANSPORT PROCESS ITSELF. IT IS DIFFICULT ENOUGH TO BEAM ABOARD A VESSEL WITH ITS SHIELDS UP--BUT TO DO SO WHEN THAT VESSEL'S SHIELD HARMONICS MAY BE DIFFERENT FROM THOSE WE ARE FAMILIAR WITH--

I KNOW ALL THAT, DATA. BUT COMMANDER KROGH WAS NOT ABOUT TO HOLD HIS FIRE UNLESS I DID SOMETHING DRAMATIC--SOMETHING A KLINGON WOULD RESPECT.

PUTTING MY LIFE ON THE LINE WAS THE ONLY OPTION I HAD.
BUT YOU ARE THE CAPTAIN, SIR. YOU MUST NOT BE EXPOSED TO UNNECESSARY DANGER.

ALLOW ME TO TAKE YOUR PLACE. I CAN DO EVERYTHING YOU PLAN TO DO--AND I AM EXPENDABLE.

I APPRECIATE YOUR DEDICATION TO DUTY, DATA--BUT IF THE KLINGONS REALIZED I WAS SENDING SOME-ONE ELSE, THEY WOULD BELIEVE I AM NOT AS CONFIDENT AS I APPEAR. AND THAT WOULD BE DISASTROUS.
ANY LUCK, MISTER O'BRIEN?

I THINK I'VE FOUND A FREQUENCY THAT WILL GET YOU THROUGH, SIR. BUT IT'S NOT THAT SIMPLE...
34

...WITH OUR SENSORS UNABLE TO GET INSIDE THE VESSEL, I CAN'T BE CERTAIN WHERE YOU'LL MATERIALIZE. THERE'S ABOUT AN EQUAL CHANCE OF YOU SHOWING UP ON THEIR BRIDGE--OR IN A *BULKHEAD.*

A NECESSARY RISK, CHIEF. READY?
AYE, SIR.

ENERGIZE!
KEEP YOUR FINGERS CROSSED, MISTER DATA...

"...WHEREVER THE CAPTAIN IS, I HOPE HE'S NOT *REGRETTING* HIS DECISION..."
MERDE!

A HUMAN! WHERE DID HE COME FROM?
WHAT DIFFERENCE DOES IT MAKE? KILL HIM!

URAGGH!
STOP! I MEAN YOU NO HARM-- I'M HERE TO HELP!

PLEASE LISTEN! I MUST GET TO THE BRIDGE--
--OR WE'LL ALL BE DESTROYED IN A MATTER OF MINUTES!

LYING FEDERATION SCUM! HE'S JUST TRYING TO SAVE HIS HIDE!
UNNH!

LET'S SHOW HIM WHAT WE THINK OF HIS LIES!

NO. THERE IS NOTHING TO GAIN BY DESTROYING HIM. LET US AT LEAST HEAR HIM OUT FIRST.
PERHAPS HE HAS INFORMATION WE CAN PUT TO GOOD USE.

IN ANY EVENT, HE MAY BE USED AS A BARGAINING CHIP-- TO EFFECT OUR RELEASE. I AGREE-- LET THE HUMAN SPEAK.

MY NAME IS PICARD. I'M THE CAPTAIN OF THE FEDERATION SHIP ENTERPRISE, WHICH IS ALL THAT STANDS RIGHT NOW BETWEEN THIS VESSEL AND A HALF-DOZEN KLINGON BATTLE CRUISERS!

WHAT ARE YOU SAYING? THAT WE'RE HOME?
YOU'RE IN THE HEART OF THE KLINGON EMPIRE. BUT THE KLINGONS DON'T KNOW WHAT TO MAKE OF YOU. THEY THINK YOU'RE INVADERS.

THEN ALL WE NEED DO IS SHOW OURSELVES. THEY'LL SEE WHO WE ARE!
I DON'T THINK THAT'S POSSIBLE--OR THOSE ON THE BRIDGE WOULD HAVE DONE IT ALREADY. SOMETHING MAY BE WRONG WITH YOUR COMMUNICATIONS SYSTEM.

I HAVE ARRANGED A SIGNAL WITH THE KLINGON COMMANDER IN CHARGE OF THOSE BATTLE CRUISERS--A SIGNAL THAT WILL SHOW HIM YOU MEAN NO HARM. BUT UNLESS I CAN REACH YOUR BRIDGE, HE'LL NEVER RECEIVE IT--
--AND HE'LL BE FORCED TO DESTROY US.

WHY WOULD THE EMPIRE NEED YOUR HELP? INDEED, WHY WOULD THEY TRUST YOU ANY MORE THAN THEY TRUST US?
I CAN SEE IT'S BEEN SOME TIME SINCE YOU'VE BEEN IN CONTACT WITH YOUR PEOPLE. THE KLINGONS AND THE FEDERATION ARE ALLIES.
THAT WOULD EXPLAIN THE PRESENCE OF THAT KLINGON WHO FOUGHT US-- THE ONE WHO SITS NOW ON THE BRIDGE.
IT SEEMS THIS PICARD MAY BE TELLING THE TRUTH.
BUT IF WE ARE IN THE KLINGON EMPIRE-- WHAT GOOD DOES THAT DO MY PEOPLE? WHERE'S THE PROFIT IN LETTING YOU GO, PICARD--WHEN WE COULD USE YOU AS A HOSTAGE?
YOU DIDN'T HEAR ME. IN A FEW MINUTES, THE KLINGONS WILL BLOW THIS SHIP UP--WHETHER I'M ABOARD OR NOT.
UNLESS, OF COURSE, IT BLOWS ITSELF UP FIRST.
THE CHOICE IS YOURS--SURVIVAL OR DESTRUCTION. BUT YOU'VE GOT TO MAKE IT NOW.
IT WOULD BE SATISFYING INDEED TO TEAR YOU LIMB FROM LIMB. BUT IF YOU ARE TELLING THE TRUTH...

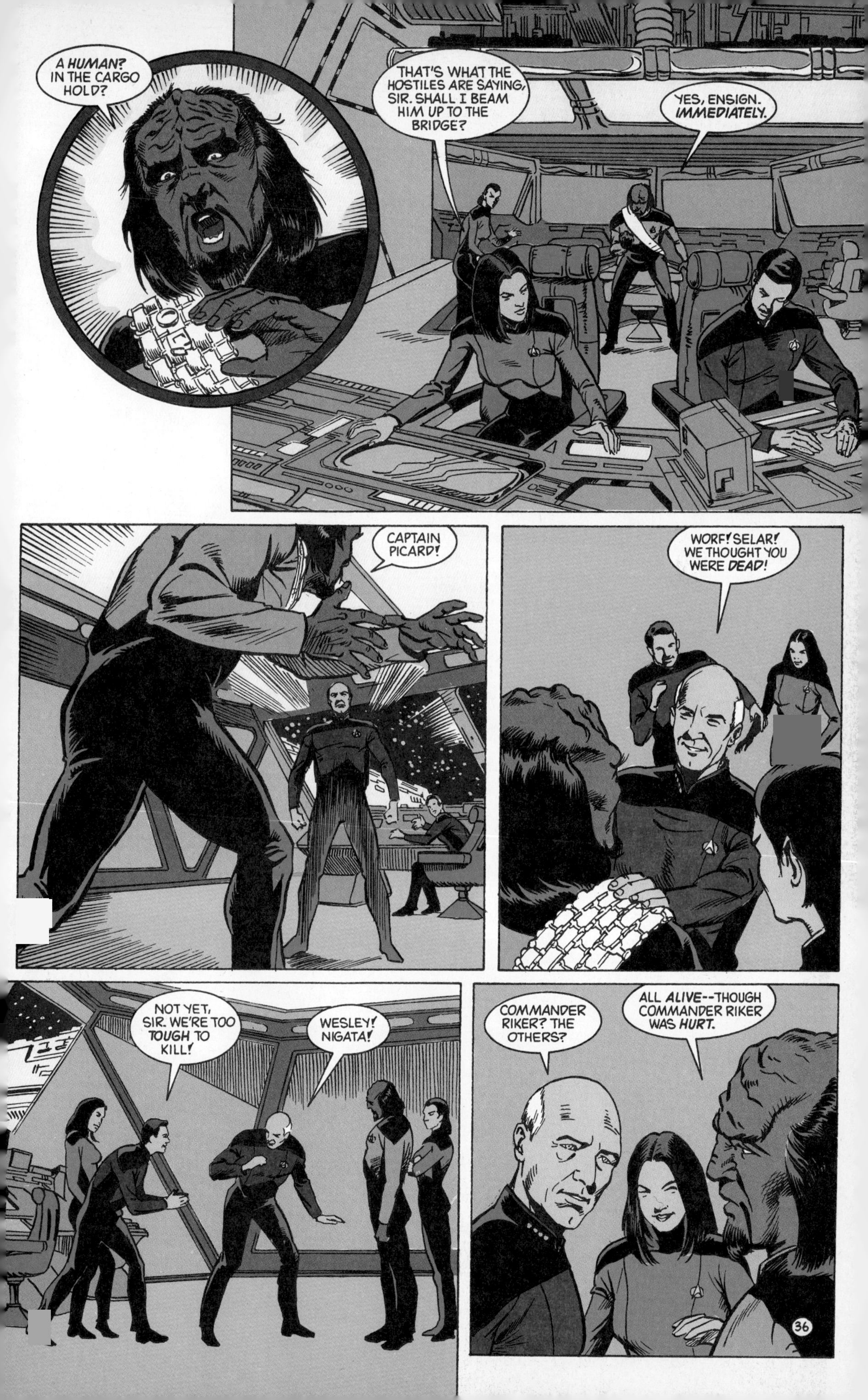

A *HUMAN?* IN THE CARGO HOLD?
THAT'S WHAT THE HOSTILES ARE SAYING, SIR. SHALL I BEAM HIM UP TO THE BRIDGE?
YES, ENSIGN. *IMMEDIATELY.*

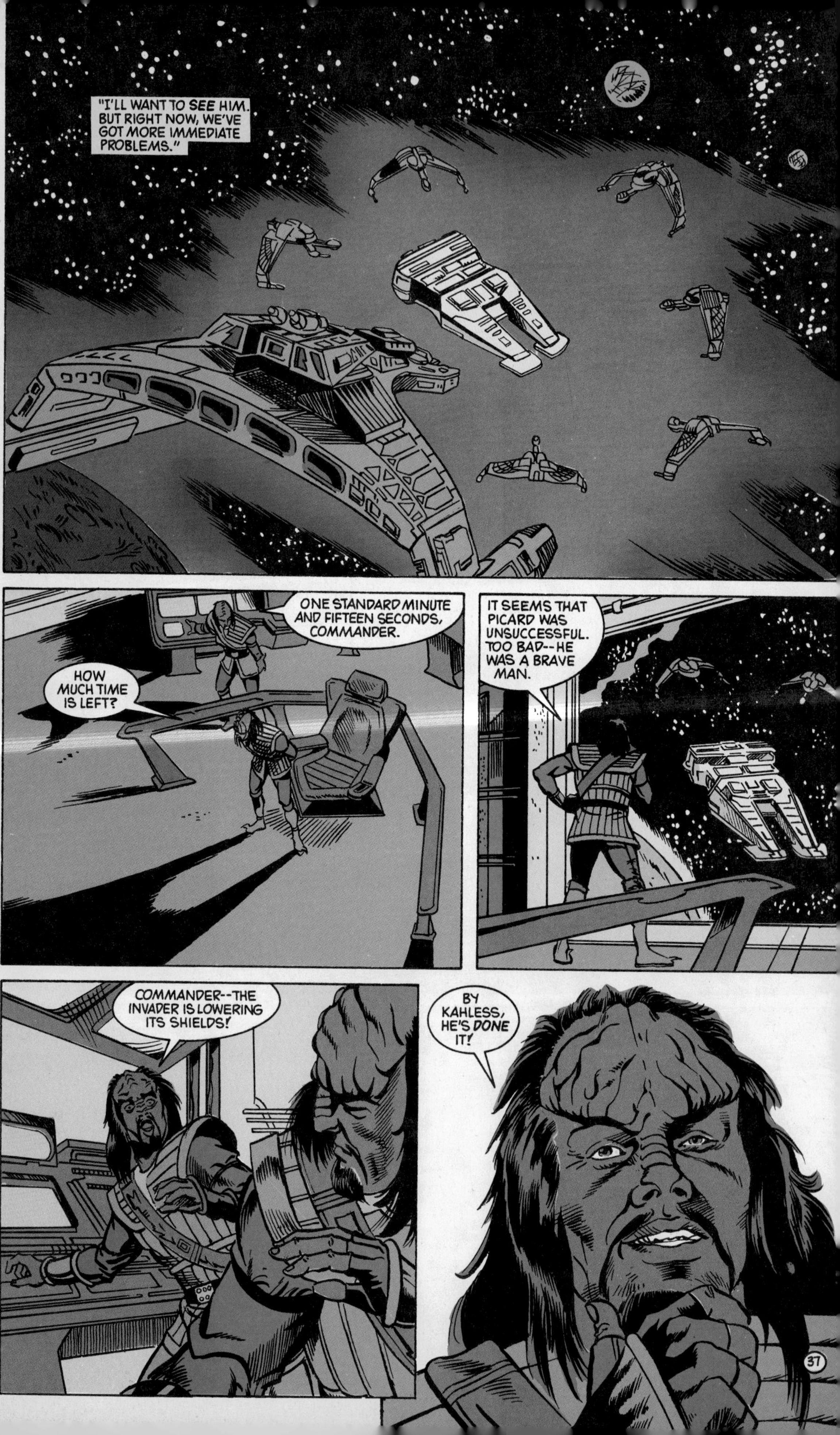

"I'LL WANT TO *SEE* HIM. BUT RIGHT NOW, WE'VE GOT MORE IMMEDIATE PROBLEMS."

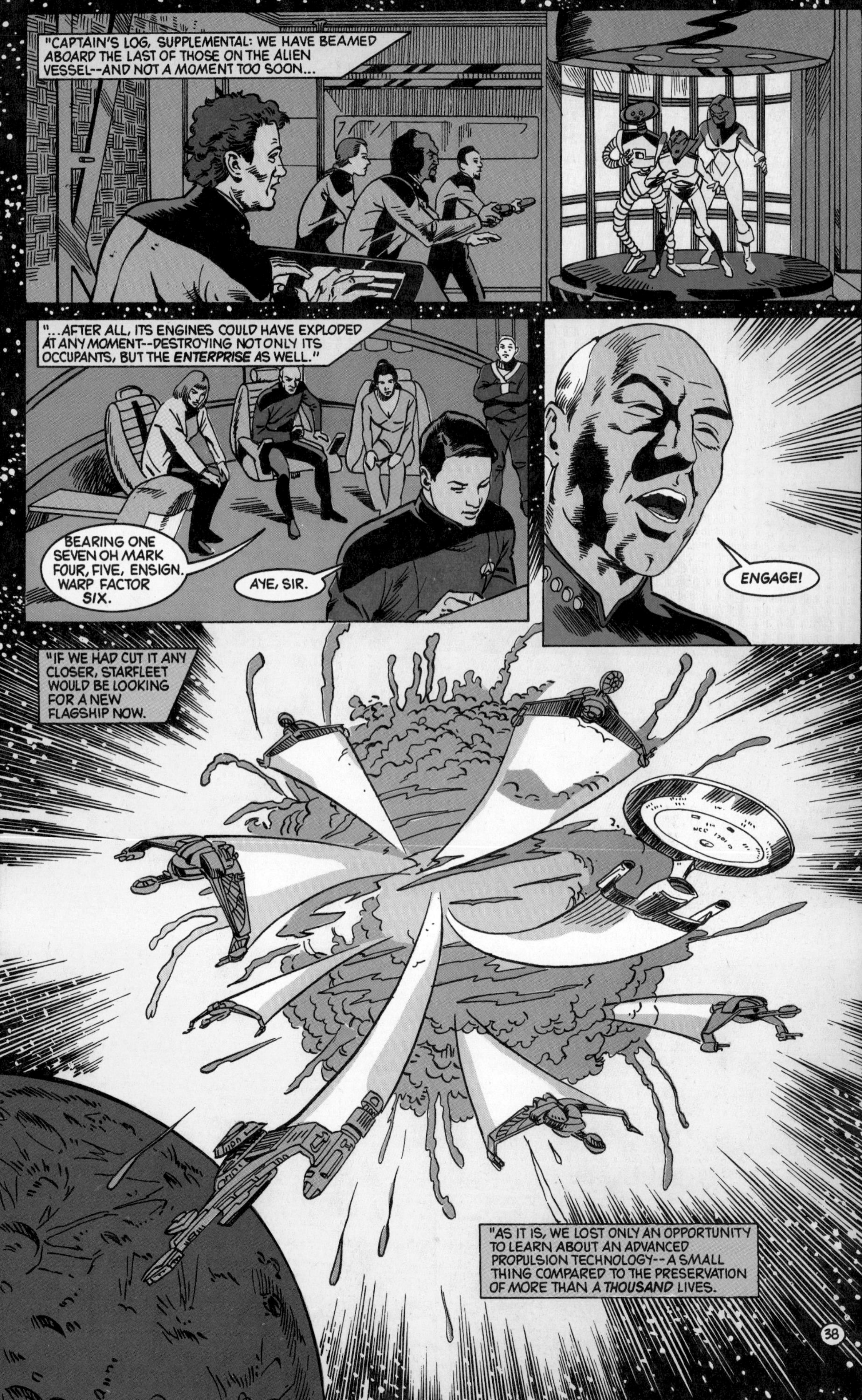
"CAPTAIN'S LOG, SUPPLEMENTAL: WE HAVE BEAMED ABOARD THE LAST OF THOSE ON THE ALIEN VESSEL--AND NOT A MOMENT TOO SOON...
"...AFTER ALL, ITS ENGINES COULD HAVE EXPLODED AT ANY MOMENT--DESTROYING NOT ONLY ITS OCCUPANTS, BUT THE ENTERPRISE AS WELL."
BEARING ONE SEVEN OH MARK FOUR, FIVE, ENSIGN. WARP FACTOR SIX.
AYE, SIR.
ENGAGE!
"IF WE HAD CUT IT ANY CLOSER, STARFLEET WOULD BE LOOKING FOR A NEW FLAGSHIP NOW.
"AS IT IS, WE LOST ONLY AN OPPORTUNITY TO LEARN ABOUT AN ADVANCED PROPULSION TECHNOLOGY--A SMALL THING COMPARED TO THE PRESERVATION OF MORE THAN A THOUSAND LIVES.

"A COMMENDATION IS IN ORDER FOR LIEUTENANT WORF, WHOSE COURAGE AND LEADERSHIP ENABLED THE CREW OF THE EINSTEIN TO FIND ITS WAY HOME.

"LIKEWISE, DOCTOR SELAR, WHO KEPT MY FIRST OFFICER ALIVE DESPITE THE MOST ADVERSE OF CIRCUMSTANCES--

"--AND ENSIGN WESLEY CRUSHER, WHOSE HELMSMANSHIP AND NAVIGATIONAL SKILLS PROVED INVALUABLE. LET THE RECORD SHOW THAT I AM VERY PROUD OF THIS YOUNG MAN.

"NATURALLY, DARIOS APPOLENE AND HIS PEOPLE WILL BE RETURNED TO THEIR VARIOUS WORLDS--WHICH MAY MAY HAVE CHANGED A BIT SINCE THEY SAW THEM LAST.

"THEY WILL NEED TO ADJUST--A TASK IN WHICH THEY WILL BE AIDED BY ENSIGN NIGATA, DOCTORS GOLD AND MARINO AND NURSE FARADAY, WHO HAVE VOLUNTEERED THEIR FREE TIME TO EXPEDITE THE LEARNING PROCESS.

"AS FOR THE HOSTILES... THEY TOO MUST BE RETURNED TO THEIR POINTS OF ORIGIN. OF COURSE, THIS WILL REQUIRE THE COORDINATED EFFORTS OF MANY STARFLEET VESSELS. IT WOULD BE INEFFICIENT TO HAVE THE ENTERPRISE FERRY THEM ALL HOME."

"CAPTAIN'S PERSONAL LOG: AS THE MAN RESPONSIBLE FOR THIS STARSHIP, I HAVE BEEN TRAINED TO BE OBJECTIVE IN ALL SITUATIONS-- INCLUDING THOSE THAT INVOLVE THE LOSS OF OFFICERS AND CREWPEOPLE.

"I WAS *NOT* OBJECTIVE IN THE MATTER OF THE EINSTEIN. I PERSISTED IN BELIEVING THAT MY PEOPLE WERE ALIVE--DESPITE ALL EVIDENCE TO THE CONTRARY.

"IS THIS A FLAW IN MY PERSONALITY-- IN MY ABILITY TO COMMAND? I DO NOT BELIEVE SO. I AM A CAPTAIN, BUT I AM ALSO A MAN--AND MUST ON OCCASION LISTEN TO MY HEART.

"THE TRUTH IS, I HAVE COME TO THINK OF THOSE WHO SERVE UNDER ME AS MY *FAMILY*.

"AND IT IS A GREAT COMFORT TO ME THAT MY FAMILY IS ONCE AGAIN *INTACT*.
"I AM ETERNALLY GRATEFUL TO THE FATES THAT MADE IT SO."
THE END

COVER GALLERY

STAR TREK
THE NEXT GENERATION
STAR TREK: THE NEXT GENERATION
23
FRIEND
F.O.E?
BY FRIEDMAN, KRAUSE AND MARCOS

STAR TREK
THE NEXT GENERATION
STAR TREK: THE NEXT GENERATION
22
SURROUNDED!
BY FRIEDMAN, KRAUSE AND MARCOS

STAR TREK
THE NEXT GENERATION
STAR TREK: THE NEXT GENERATION
24
48-page
ANNIVERSARY ISSUE

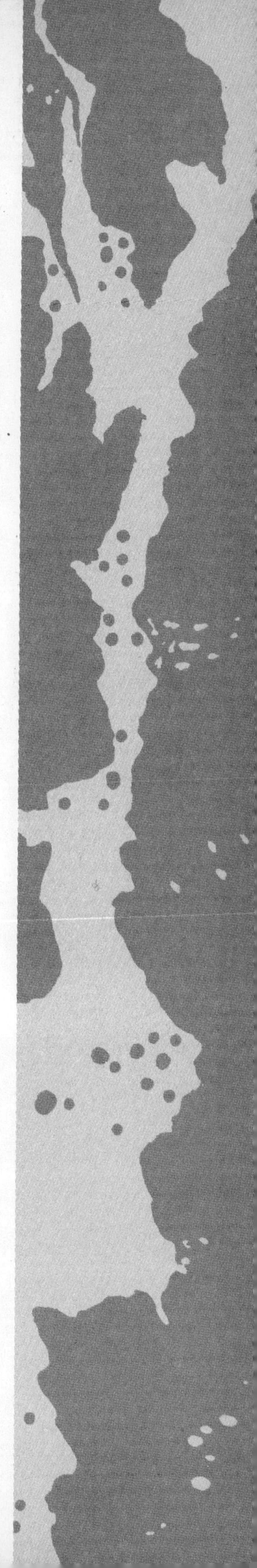

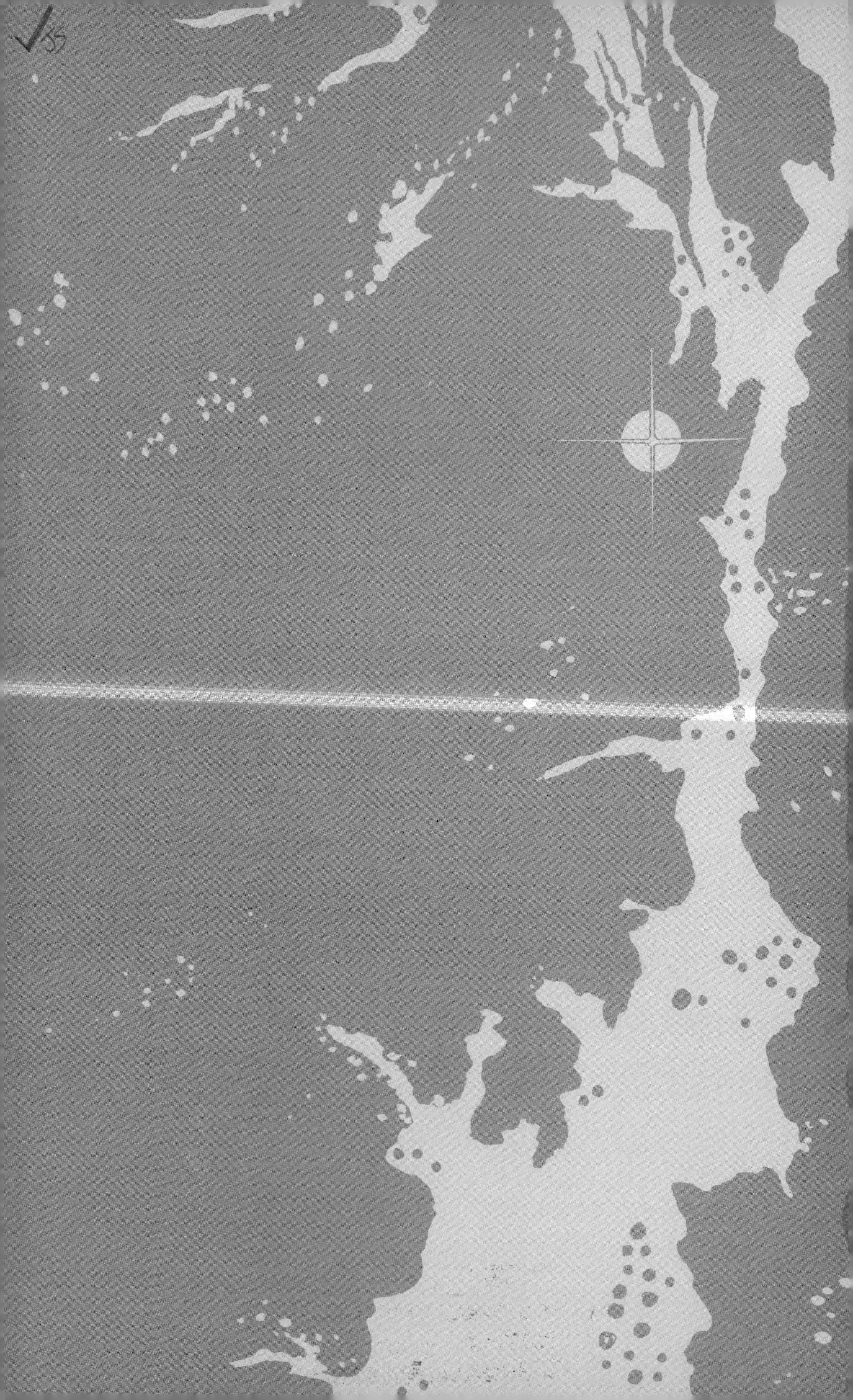